Don't Leave Me Alone

by

Kishan Lal Sharma

Double9 BOOKS

Don't Leave Me Alone

by Kishan Lal Sharma

ISBN: 978-93-59323-60-2

Published by

DOUBLE 9 BOOKS
2/13-B, Ansari Road
Daryaganj, New Delhi – 110002
info@double9books.com
www.double9books.com
Tel. 011-40042856

ABOUT THE AUTHOR

Kishan Lal Sharma, born on July 18, 1950, in Mehsana, Gujarat, is a multifaceted author renowned for his contributions to literature. He is the son of Smt. Chand Devi and Sri Ram Pal Sharma and is married to Indra Sharma. His educational journey includes earning a B.A. degree and a Diploma in story and screenplay writing. Sharma's literary journey began with his first work, "Rashifal," a collection of satire and taunts, published in Diwana Tej in 1978. Over the years, he has received recognition and acclaim, earning the prestigious title of Vidyavachaspati by Vikramshila Hindi Vidyapeeth, Bhagalpur in 2014 for his contributions to teaching. His writing spans across diverse genres, including stories, articles, poetry, novels, and short stories (Laghukathya), as well as reviews. Sharma's work has found a home in esteemed publications like Amar Ujala, Rajasthan Patrika, Ajit Samachar, and many more, with a consistent presence since 1978. Among his notable publications, his novel "Hara Hua Aadmi" stands out, showcasing his storytelling prowess. Additionally, his works have been featured in numerous collections, such as Laghukatha Sansar, Andhaimod, and Bharat Nepal Laghuratha Darpan, to name just a few. Kishan Lal Sharma's literary journey is a testament to his dedication and versatility as an author, and his contributions continue to enrich the world of literature with his insightful and thought-provoking writings.

CONTENTS

About this book

My writing started in the year 1978 with the publication of a satire and taunt story in a magazine published from Delhi. And after this my writing started getting published in Hindi. Newspaper and Magazines of the country and the states.

And the process of writing and publishing continues even today.

A Novel has been published in these last years, My writing works have been complied in many collections. I have also published three story books and four Laghukrthas collections.

At the time of Lockdown the idea come to my mind to translate my Hindi stories into English.

And my first book of poems in English which was Don't touch me, was published by Astitva Prakashan-Bilaspur, Chhattisgarh. This book is also available on Flipkart and Amazon.

"Don't Leave me Alone", is my second book in English. It is a book of stories. It has different colours of life. In these stories there is love, there is hate, there is displacement from one's country, there is patriotism, there is love for husband and wife, there is also terrorism.

The title story, Don't leave me alone", is based on a fantasy that might happen sometime in the future.

The stories in this collection will entertain as well as give a message. With this hope is in your hands.

Your suggestions, thoughts and feedback is invaluable to me. I will be waiting.

Forgive me

"Please forgive me. I sincerely apologize to you while doing this I did not think that your social reputation will be shocked. What will happen on your heart."

"But Why did you do such a hideous, Stupid act?" Julia's face turned red as soon as she saw that man.

"My friend bet me. In the process of winning the bet, I did Such a ridiculous, disgusting act".

Football world cup matches were going on. Standing In front of the Camera, Julia was broadcasting the match live. Then suddenly a young man pounced on her like an eagle. He takes Julia in his arms, and kissed her lips.

Julia was reporter for many years in the TV channel of her country Colombia, But for the first time she got a chance to come on foreign soil. She came to Russia to broadcast football world cup matches. The young man had quickly left before Julia Could understand anything.

She was nervous due to a sudden incident. The vigor, enthusiasm should be in the reporter while broadcasting the match. It was not while airing the rest of the match.

She was deeply disappointed by the incident of sexual harreshment in public place. The video of that incident was going viral on social media. The incident of sexual harreshment with a foreign woman reporter should not spoil the image of the police. To avoid this the police found and arrested the accused. The police brought the culprit to Julia.

"Now you are apologizing. Do not think before doing such a hideous act, my social reputation will be clouded. What will happen on my heart?

"I wanted to win a bet with my friend. So I forgot all."

"If someone from your sister, daughter or wife did this act"? Julia threw question at him.

"So I would teach him such a lesson that in life he would not dare to do this again to any woman." He was angry after listening to Julia.

"You are very concerned about the honor of your sister, daughter and wife. Not mine I am also someone's sister, daughter"?

Julia also got angry after seeing her gesture, "You are talking about punishing a man who has done such a wrong act with your sister or daughter. And you apologize to me for such a malicious act with me. You too should be punished. So that in future you also can not dare to do this with any woman."

"Come on", after listening to Julia, the police officer told him.

Now they had gone a few steps ahead that Julia said. "Officer this man is not able to forgive. It should be severaly punished. He deserves punishment ... but...

"But ... what ..."? listening to her police officer stopped.

"Its action has made me a film star overnight and my carrer on top", Julia said.

"This man is not worthy of forgiveness I still forgive him."

Selfie

"Will go alone?" Nazia spoke holding Shiva's hand.

Shiva was very upset to here the news of Riya's wedding. He did not even think in his dream that Riya could do this too. Riya promised to marry him but was married to Rohan. He was so hurt by Riya's infidelity that after deciding in his heart, he went behind Bandra Fort.

In order to execute the decision in mind, he started moving towards the high rocks on the sea shore. He was walking slowly thinking about Riya's infidelity. That's when he heard the sound of girls blossoming. He looked up.

Nisha, Meera and Nazia were friends. They came to have a picnic. They were singing, dancing and having fun. Suddenly Nazia said, "I take a selfie."

She moved to the edge of the rock to take a selfie. She took the mobile in front of her. There was a lot of water behind her back. As soon as she was about to click, all of sudden high-pitched wave broke out in the sea. The velocity of the waves was so fast hit that rock when she returned, she took Nazia away.

Meera and Nisha shouted loudly as nazia fell in to the sea, "help.... help. "

As soon as she fell in to the sea. She started screaming as she hit her hands in the water, Midday. The sea shore was deserted. Apart from those girls there was only Shiva. Shiva was stunned for a while seeing this scene Nisha and Meera constantly screaming for help. Hearing those voices, the Shiva ran quickly and leaped in to the sea.

The sea was turbulent. The high roar was rising with terrible roar. Nazia was to be rescued from the sea by swiming against the waves. Nazia's screaming voices were constantly coming. Going in the direction of the voice, Shiva tries to find her. After some time her voice stopped coming. Shiva felt like seeing the waves rising in the sea. Do not die in the process of saving her. But he came here with this intention when he must die, do the right thing before he dies.

Nizia could not see, but he not did give up. He was constantly trying to find Nazia amidst the rising waves in the sea. Eventually his hard work paid off. He managed to find her. He brought her out of the sea.

He laid Nazia on the ground. Then he had to squeeze her stomatch. She was unconscious. Even after a lot of effort she did not become conscious. Then he took her to the hospital. Nazia's condition was critical. After a lot of efforts by doctors she was brought to consciousness. As soon as she regained consciousness, she said. " I had fallen in to sea, who saved me"?

"Shiva", pointing to Nisha said, "If there was no Shiva today "

"Thank God. He sent you to save me an angel", Nazia said thankfully.

"I am not an angel", Shiva said, "If there was someone else, he would have done the same thing that I have done".

"Did you also come to have a picnic"? Nazia asked him.

"No", he said, "I came with the intention of suicide."

"Atmhatya means suicide", Nazia spoke with surprise after listening to him. "But why do you want to commit suicide."

I was in love with Riya. She also wanted me. She had also promised marriage. But she infidelized me and married a rich man. Shiva told Nazia the reason for suicide.

"Riya loved money not you". Nazia hearing the story of Shiva said, "You were going to commit suicide because of a girl who does not love you? I can't imagine a brave man like you doing such a cowardly act."

"You opened my eyes. What was I going to do. I would have been dead today if you hadn't", Shiva said after listening to Nazia, "Now you are fine. I will go?

"Will you go alone"? Shiva asked to go, then Nazia said, "Riya had committed infidelity with you, but I will not".

"I did not understand what you want to say"?

"Today if you don't save me. I would not be in this world. You have saved my life. I entrust myself to you.

Shiva did not even think that this will happen to him. He came to die. But with life, life partner was also found.

Search for missing husband abroad

The Sun was setting slowly behind distant hills. The rays of the setting Sun created amazing views in the snow-cupped hills. Seeing that scene Ranjan said, " You sit on this stone".

"Why"? Mrinali saw Ranjan from question point of view.

"The horizon is red with the rays of the Sun falling behind your back, put your hand on your cheek and sit on a stone thinking about some thing. How beautiful your pose will be".

Mrinali had to sit at Ranjan's behest. Ranjan took poses in different styles of Mrinali. He had to be back and forth to take every pose. He was so engrossed in photographing that he did not feel that he had come to the end of the hill. As soon as he was careless his foot slipped and a scream erupted in the valley.

Mrinali ran to catch to Ranjan screaming. But in vain, Ranjan fell in to the river flowing down the valley. Mrinali acted sensibly with patience. She immediately informed Police. But in vain, the police tried to find Ranjan, but his body was not found.

This accident happened five year ago. People believed that Ranjan is not in this world. But Mrinali was not ready to accept this. She believed that if Ranjan had died, his body would have been found. But it did not happen. It can also mean Ranjan is alive. But if he is alive. So where is he?

Even after five years, Mrinali did not forget that accident. So she used to come to that place after taking leave from the company again and again from where Ranjan fell in the river. Even today where Ranjan had fallen, Mrinali was standing there and watching carefully the river flowing in the valley. For some time she stood there. Then she slowly crossed the slope and came to an open level.

An old man was sitting on a stone by the river. He was thinking something. Mrinali stopped walking. After looking at the old man for a while, She asked, "Baba, what are you thinking about?"

"Remembering those days when I bathed in the river. I used to go across. But now can't go."

"Why can't go now".

"Now that part of the river is under the possession of Pakistan."

"If some thing floats away from here"? Mrinali asked after listening him.

"The man over there will take." "If there is a man?"

"How can some one take a man?"

"If the man accidently falls in to the river and faints or dies."

"Then it will be something else", the old man said, "but why are you asking this?"

Mrinali narrated the whole incident on the old man asking. Hearing Mrinali the old man said, "daughter, don't worry. I will help you in searching for your husband."

"How Baba"?

"The army is not deployed on all the routes to go to that side. I know the way that I can go there. I will take you there."

"When Baba"?

"You come to this place tonight."

Mrinali reached the same place at night. Rasool was already waiting for her. After crossing the rocky path, forest and snow covered hills in the dark, they reached a village in occupied Kashmir. Rasool knocked on the door of a house.

"Who are"? The door of the house was also opened with this question.

"Rasool. You"? Ghulam Ali said with surprise when he saw the man standing in front. "Have you forgotten the way today? You just stopped comming here."

"Due to the terrorists, it has become very tough now. It is not easy to come here. Due to this daughter, I had to come today."

"Who is she? why did you have to come?"

"Will you asked the whole thing by standing outside? or will you take us in?"

"Sorry", Ghulam Ali realized his mistake. He took them in. "Sit and now tell everything."

"She is Mrinali. Her husband is missing." Rasool said while introducing Mrinali, "What happened to you that day? Narrate the whole incident."

Mrinali narrated the entire incident of that day to Ghulam Ali. Ghulam Ali said after listening to her, "No man was found dead or alive in this village. I will go to nearby villages and find out."

Ghulam Ali left home. He went to many nearby villages. He returned in the evening.

"What did you know about Ranjan?" Mrinali asked eagerly after seeing Ghulam Ali.

"Daughter, Sirajuddin of Rajori village found a man lying unconscious in the river five years ago." Ghulam Ali told the whole thing.

"Where is he now?" Mrinali asked.

"That man had lost his memory. Who is he? Where is he from? That man did not remember. Sirajuddin was childless. He accepted him as his son." Ghulam Ali told Mrinali about that man.

"You met that man?"

"Sirajuddin had married his son Irfan two year ago to a girl from England. The condition of the relationship was, Irfan will have to go England. Sirajuddin also went to England after the son's mariage."

Mrinali could not get more information about Irfan. She came back to Delhi.

Who is Irfan? How to meet him? Many such question emerged in his mind. After many days of thinking, she decided to go to England. Mrinali served in the multi national company. She got her transfer to England.

Mrinali went to England. There she tried to find out which girl is married to a Pakistani Youth. But this did not help her find Irfan. Whenever Mrinali finds time, she starts searching for Irfan. She wanted to know whether Irfan and Ranjan are not the same man. She was also moving to other cities for her search.

One day Mrinali came out of a shop then she looked at a man. His face looked like Ranjan when viewed from a distance. Mrinali ran towards that young man. But Mrinali could reach him, before that the young man sat in the car. The car left but Mrinali had read the car number. Mrinali went to registration office to find out about the car. She finds out the car is registered in the name of Ramjan. Ramjan lives in Winchester. Mrinali reached Ramjan's House one day.

"Whom do you want to meet "? Seeing Mrinali, a woman asked her. "Is it the house of Ramjan"

"Yes."

"Who are you? What is your relationship with Ramjan."

"I am his daughter Saira."

"Are you married to Pakistani Youth Irfan." Mrinali asked saira.

"Yes , but why are you asking?"

Mrinali said while introducing herself, "I want to meet your husband"

"My husband is just about to come. Please come inside." Saira starts talking to Mrinali in the drawing room.

when they were both talking. Then Saira got a call from someone.

"What-where?" Saira asked after hearing the phone. And Saira ran away from hearing the stranger's voice. Mrinali also went with her. They both reached the hospital. Saira met the doctor. The doctor said, " Nothing to worry. It is a minor injury."

Saira went to ward, Mrinali was also went with her.

"What happened?"

"Nothing to worry."

"She wants to meet you." Saira told her husband.

Irfan's eyes on Mrinali. He felt like seeing seen her before. Where did see her? When he stressed his mind, he felt like his brain would explode. And he started seeing something blurred in the distant past. And after a while, suddenly a name came out of his tongue, "Mrinali? You?"

"Ranjan", And Mrinali said hugging him", I believed you are alive. And today won my trust."

"I was conscious when I fell down the mountain. My head hit a stone, when I fell in the river. Then I can't remember anything, but seeing you in front of me today. The last thing I forgot is now remembering one by one."

Saira was shocked to see this scene. She could not understand anything for a long time she remained silent spectator. After some time she said, "Do you know each other?"

"We are husband and wife."

"What are you saying."

"I am right", Irfan said

"You are married to me. Then how can you've a husband and wife?"

Saira asked after listening to Irfan.

"Let me tell you". And Mrinali remembered her past.

Ranjan and Mrinali were friends when they were studying in college. Their friendship slowly turned in to love. After completing college, they both got job in a company.

They both got married after getting a job. After marriage they wanted to go to Kashmir for honeymoon. But due to Ranjan's mother sudden illness, they had to cancell their program to go to Kashmir. So, they went to Kashmir on the first wedding anniversary.

Kashmir is called heaven on Earth. Snow capped mountains, water falls and lakes, greenery scattered in the valleys, flowers and apple trees.

They both used to go somewhere every day. Get lost in the world of love in a hotel room every night.

Mrinali was very happy to find her friend, her lover Ranjan as her husband. But God may not have accepted her happiness. One evening Mrinali and Ranjan were sitting on a hill. The Sun was setting slowly. The setting Sun created a wonderful view in to the valley.

Ranjan said after seeing that scene.

"Mrinali. you sit on this stone."

"Why? " Mrinali asked.

"You sit on this stone, the Sun behind your back. How beautiful your photo will come? "

Mrinali sat on that stone at the behest of her husband. Ranjan started taking photographs of wife's in different poses. He was so busey taking photographs that he did not notice that he had come to the end of the hills. As soon as he was careless his foot slipped and a scream erupted in the valley.

Mrinali was shocked for a while seeing the sudden incident. Then she handled herself. She called the police. Police tried a lot but Ranjan was not found. Mrinali went to Kashmir with her husband but came back alone.

"So this is Ranjan?" Saira spoke knowing Mrinali's past.

"Yes Saira this is Ranjan. I believed Ranjan is alive. Six years later my faith came true", Mrinali said, "But look at God. Ranjan found but as Irfan. He is no longer my husband. Now he is your husband."

Mrinali had gone.But there was a stir in Saira's life. Is Mrinali true? Saira called her father-in-law. Saira felt into confusion after knowing the truth from her father-in-law.

Ranjan was a resident of India. He was married to Mrinali. But an accident separated them both. He lost his memory and got a new name Irfan. Irfan was married to Saira.

Time had brought Ranjan in a strange situation. Saira was on one side, Mrinali on the other side. He was duly married to both. Who was he today Ranjan or Irfan. Saira's husband or Mrinali's. Can he forget Mrinali by staying with Saira? Not at all. Mrinali is his first love and nobody forgets their first love.

Mrinali leaves but Ranjan goes to London to meet her. He did not go by telling Saira. But Saira gets to know. A woman can never let her husband love another woman. Irfan may have been Ranjan before but now he was her husband. She had no tolerance for her husband going to Mrinali.

Saira did not want her husband to go to meet Mrinali. But Irfan did not listen to his wife. So there was a dispute between them. Mrinali came to know about this.

Mrinali spared no effort to find Ranjan. It was due to her hard work that she finally found her husband.

But even after finding her husband, she was not happy. The reason for this was Ranjan's second marriage to Saira. Saira married life was broken due to Mrinali. Mrinali was came to know about this. Then Mrinali told him,

"You don't come to me."

"Why are you refusing to come to me."

"You are now Saira's husband."

"Don't forget first I'm your husband."

"You live in my heart. I still consider you my husband. But it is also true Saira's right over you. You are her husband." Mrinali lovingly explained to Ranjan.

"I have not married Saira by name change or by fraud", Ranjan said after listening to Mrinali, "whatever happened was a coincidance".

"I agree with you", Mrinali said, "But in the eyes of the world, Ranjan is not in this world. Now you are not Ranjan. You are Irfan. And Irfan is Saira's husband."

"Call you widow while husband is alive. How is this justice. You are mine. I can't live without you."

"For my hsappiness, I can not destroy another woman house."

"I can't live without you. If Saira object to my happiness. Then I will divorce her.

Irfan also told Saira the same thing. Hearing about divorce from Irfan, she got confused. The husband who loved her heartly. After meeting Mrinali, there was a sudden change in him. Saira was deeply in love with Irfan. She can't live apart from him.

Mrinali also understand that Saira will not be happy if she stays here. So she decided to leave England. Mrinali wanted to leave England without telling Ranjan. She took her transfer back to India. One day she left for airport. Ranjan calls Mrinali. But her mobile was switchoff. Then he called his office. From there he came to know that Mrinali has been transfered to Delhi. And she is going by night flight.

He won't let Mrinali go. If she want to go then he will go with her. He also told Saira about his decision. Saira got into thinking. What should she do?

Irfan was gone. She kept thinking for a long time. And then she also left for the airport. Mrinali and Ranjan were talking when Saira reached the airport. Mrinali was telling Ranjan.

"Now you are not Ranjan. In the eyes of the world you are Irfan. And stay as Irfan."

"Now this can not happen. I am not Irfan, I am Ranjan.

"What will happen to Saira. if you become to Ranjan?"

"Mrinali whatever you say, but the truth is that I cannot live without you."

"You are going." Saira said after listening to her.

"Yes, it is right for me to leave here. It is good for all three of us." "Incidentally the same man is Ranjan and Irfan is also. This man has neither cheated you nor me. Whatever happened is the will of God."

"Saira, I agree with you. But it is also true that Irfan is your husband. Now it is only right that he remains yours."

"No. Mrinali", Saira said, "We both can get happiness only when we consider our husband's happiness as our own."

"I do not understand your talk?"

"Mrinali, Irfan can't forget you and I can't forget him." Saira said. "So we have to take a decision that is in favour of the three of us."

"What could be the decision", Mrinali asked.

"Luck has made both of us a partner. If both of us start living together then we will get our love.'

"What are you saying?"

"Telling the truth. If both of us stay together then you will get your husband Ranjan and I will get my husband. Irfan, we will both have a home and a happy world.?

And the three returned holding each other's hand.

Face book

"When are you getting married?

"Marriage"?

"What does your future husband do"?

"Marriage? Husband? I can't understand what you are saying"? She spoke after listening to him.

"You have posted on Facebook about your engagement".

"O... o... h... h... o "? When she understood the meaning of his words she said, "I posted that post just like that."

"To fool people"?

"Not to fool people. To protect myself from people."

"I did not understand what you want to say"?

"I have written a virgin in my profile. I'm virgin so people used to tease me. used to send dirty and vulgar messages on my time line." She said the reason for her post, "I had posted that post to avoid them."

"But I never did that to you." He said after listening to her.

"I know. That is why I am telling you the reality of my post."

"But if you want your post can be real."

"I did not understand what you want to say"?

"I want you. I am in love with you. Want to make you mine. I want to marry you." he had expressed his heart's desire to her.

Different countries, different religions, different culture and they never met. Only friends on facebook. The sudden marriage proposal had made her think.

Creation

them"

"Stop... Stop...You both have gone mad?" "She spoke separating

This story is a century old. The means of transport and communications were advanced. But not as many today. A ship was going from one continent to another by sea. People of different countries, races were aboard this ship. People were laughing, joking, having fun in the journey. One night there was a sudden storm in the sea. The ship could not with stand that storm. And drowned in the sea. People scream as soon as the ship sinks.

Two men leap from the sinking ship. The storm swep them away both men fainted while flowing with water. One said when he came to his senses in the morning, "where I?"

Another man looked around and then he said, "Looks like the storm has brought us to an Island."

They both remembered the night's incident for a while. Then one said, "I am hungry".

"Let's look at some food?" Second said and they went in search of food. They both came to know in a few hours. It was a deserted island. There was nothing on that island other than just wild animals and trees, plants and grass. There were a lot of fruits trees. They were both hungry. They ate the fruits from the trees.

And then they both came to beach. They waited for a ship to pass by the island. The whole day passed. But did not any ship pass near the island. The Sun sets. Darkness sperad all around. The sound of wild animals began to be heard at night. They both climbed a tree to avoid them. And thus many days passed.

Now they understand. This deserted island is cursed. Nobody comes to or around this island. They will have to spend the rest of their lives on this island. Life Cannot be lived while homeless. They have to build a house to live. Together they made a hut using trees, grass, bushes and stones which was easily available there.

In the day both went to the forest. Plucking fruits from trees. Then they used to come and set on the beach. They still had not given up hope. They were confident that some ship would come here one day. But every day they disappointed.

Some times some stuff comes to the shore. If it was of their use, they would bring it.

Gradually, the days passed as month. And the months passed as year.

Many years later, one day when both of them reached the beach, they were surprised to see the scene there. A girl was lying on the beach. Then they reached near her. The girl was unconscious. The girl come to her sense through their efforts. She said as soon as she regained consciousness. "Where I?"

"You are on a deserted island". One told her.

Another asked, "How did you come here? What happened to you"?

"With me"? and she remembered the night's accident.

She was going from one continent to another by ship. There was many people on board. The ship was moving forward stopping at different ports. Every one was very happy. Every one was laughing, dancing, singing and enjoying the cruise. A sudden sea storm came at night.

Strong wind blows. The sea began to roar fier cely. Due to the waves in the sea, the ship started hitching. And finally the ship sank. Seeing the ship sink, people should starts making sound of save. But who comes there to save them.

Fast wave took her away. She fainted with fear.

"Your story is similar to ours". One said after listening to her.

gone".

"Now our numbr is three". The other said. "I won't be here".

"So what will you do"?

"If any ship comes here. I will leave".

"It's wretched island. No ship comes here. Otherwise we would have

She didn't believe their words. But after a few days, she was convinced that she would have to live on this island. And she started living with those two men.

One of those man was black and the other was white. Black and white struggle is old. White consider themeselve to be of high breed and black are of low breed. White hate black. In many countries, the struggle between whites and blacks is at its peak.

That white man also considered himself as best. Did not even allow black people to come near. But luck had brought him down with black.

The black man was his companion on this deserted island. He had to live with. They both started living together in love. There was no quarrel or dispute between them

But after the woman arrvied on the island, disputes started between them. The white man wanted to mold her is his thoughts. He wanted to make her his. The black man also wanted the same. They had to fight daily to make that woman their own And today their fight had turned into a bloody struggle.

"Why are you fighting?" She had asked.

"You are mine." white man said.

"Not his you are mine". Black man said

"You both are fighting for me". She said.

"Do you Know what will be the. result of your bloody strnggle.?"

"What will happen?" Both of them started looking at her.

"You will both be killed in this bloody struggle. And I will be left alone on this deserted island." She said explaining them, "You Know what God wants?"

"What?" both spoke together.

"God wants to populate this deserted island. So he first sent you both. Only a woman can create. So he sent me here too. But if, you both kill each other how will, God's will be done", She said, "Every problem is solved not by Conflict but by love".

"What is the solution to this problem?" They both asked.

"Why are you fighting for me. I am ready to be both".

Both of them liked her suggestion and they both live with her in love

The Foundation

Despite not wanting, Vijai and meena had to bow. to the daughter stubbornness. They had to get ready to marry their daughter to Rahul.

Neerja was a doctor. She served in a hospital. She did not get even a single minute of rest in the hospital during the day. She would breathe a sigh of relief when she came home at night. When lying in bed at night, she definitely took mobile in her hand. She definitely saw facebook, Twiter, messenger etc.

One day she got Rahul's friend request from Australia on facebook. She checked Rahul's profile. He was a doctor and was serving in a hospital. Neerja was a doctor herself, so she accepted his request.

After becoming friends, they started chatting everyday. Initially both of them used to talk personally. Later they started telling each other their hospital activities. Even small things started sharing among themselves sometimes the hours passed and their chat did not end. While chatting to Rahul, do not know when Neerja started loving him. She dreamed of making him her life partner. While chatting, she had realized that Rahul has also started liking her. Love her. Neerja was educated and open minded. But was a woman also Indian woman, She could not initiate her own marriage due to shame, hesitance and hesitation. Like every Indian girl, She also wanted the marriage proposal came from Rahul. Rahul proposed her.

One day her wish was fulfilled. One day Rahul spoke to her while chatting, "I want you Love you".

"Me too." Neerja said after listening to him.

"I want to make you mine, I want to marry you."

How long has Neerja been waiting for this proposal. So without delaying a moment, She accepted Rahul's proposal.

Neerja told her parents about Rahul.

"Who is his father? What is the introduction of his family?" Meena asked after listening to her daughter.

"Where is the age reached and you are entangled in things like Caste and family. I want to marry Rahul." Neerja spoke after listening to her mother. "Daughter I accept you but the boy is in Australia neither is there any relative of ours nor is it possible to go there for investigation Know what he is saying right"? Vijai expressed doubt after listening to his daughter.

"Papa, Rahul is telling the truth. I have been associated with him on facebook for a long time."

"Daughter is not completely true as seen on facebook." Vijai wanted to convince his daughter.

"Papa, I too care about my future. I have taken. Rahul's test in every way whatever he is saying. All Right."

Every parent worries about their daughter's future. Every parent wants to hand their daughter over to a man who deserves it Take care of their daughter. That's why every parent conducts a through investigation before their daughter's relationship. Vijai and Meena also wanted to find out Rahul's reality. But daughter's stubbornness ....

Vijai Conforms daughter's relationship by talking to Rahul over phone Rahul had said it clearly, "It is not possible to visit India for more than two days. Hence the marriage formalities have to be settled with in two days."

Vijai had no choice. Rahul came to India and married Neerja and took her with him.

Rahul leaves home early and returns late at night. One day Neerja said to him, "I want to see your hospital I also want to work in your hospital."

"See the hospital. Do your practice too what is the hurry now"?

And it happened that day. It was a talk for a long time again. whenever Neerja asks to go to the hospital with him. Rahul makes some excuse. When Rahul kept making excuses repeatedly one day Neerja followed him to his hospital.

Knowing the truth in the hospital, the foundation of her spouse was shaken. His father told him, "What is seen on facebook is not true".

What her father said was true. Rahul was not a doctor. He was a Compounder. He had created a profile that was false. He kept lying to her even more.

Relationship whose foundation is laid on lies and deception should be kept. Neerja was thinking.

Divided Love

"Nalini, are you not feeling well?"

"Yes sir, No sir, Sir I am quite well", as soon as she entered the chamber, the boss's unexpected question stung her tongue." Sir, I am quie well".

"Read it if you're OK" the letter Nalini had typed Boss threw it angrily.

Nalini takes the letter lying on the table when she read her own typed letter she was very sorry. She make mistake like live to love, see to sex while typing the letter. Because of the spelling mistake, the letter had changed. After reading her own typed letter, she did not dare to look at her boss.

"Now you have seen the sample of your typed letter".

"Yes sir", Nalini rising her neck hesitantly, "I am sorry sir"?

"This is not the first time today. You have been here for two month. You have been making similiar mistakes since you came". Boss said scolding, Nalini.

"Sir. I amreally sorry." Nalini begrudginglysaid, " Sir, I will not make such mistake further."

Ignoring Nalini's talk the boss said, "Quit if you don't feel like working. There is a lot of unemployment in the country. Give a chance to someone in need. "Sir, no such mistake again." Nalini's eyes filled with apologies to the boss.

"OK. Today I forgive you but don't make such mistakes further", Boss said warning Nalini, "Retype this letter".

Nalini felt as if her theft was caught innocently while getting out of the boss's chamber and sitting in her seat. So many mistakes oops. What would the boss even think about her? Do not make any assumptions about her ability in his mind.

After sitting in her seat, Nalini looked up and saw. The office workers were only towards her. Everyone was staring at her. Looking at the men's eyes, she felt as if their eyes were eager to see her body hidden behind the clothes.

"What happened Nalini? did you type a mistake?" Deven and Nalini's seat was close by.

"Yes". Nalini had been in this office for two months. Two month later, for the first time, a male colleague took the initiative to talk to her. "If you don't mind I say one thing".

"What?" Nalini took a closer look at Deven.

"I have been watching since you came. It looks like you are very upset. Stay sad and lost all the time. May be you have a personal problem. But what does the office have to do with your personal problem. After coming to office, forget your personal problem and think about the office. Only then you will be able to work properly. Otherwise you will keep making mistakes." Deven advised Nalini as a true friend.

"You are right'. Nalini spoke after listening the Deven.

Nalini changed a lot after that day. This happened after Deven explained. When she came to the office two months ago no one dared to talk to her after seeing her nature. But once Deven took the initiative to talk to her that Nalini also started speaking.

One evening everyone left the office. Deven said looking towards Nalini. "Don't you have to go home today".

"I will take some more time at finish my work".

"Get the rest done tomorrow".

"Just have to. As soon as the office comes in the morning, the boss has to give the typed letter.

"I help you" Deven proposed.

"Is it a matter of one day. Such opportunities will keep coming again and again. How long will you waste your time for me", Nalini saw Deven while typing.

"At the moment, I am talking about today'.

"What will other people think when they know you helped me?It should not have a bad effect on the boss?" Nalini said hesitantly.

"It is not wrong to ask the partner about the work of the office or seek his help". Deven said, "Don't be afraid I am with you".

"If you say so?" Nalini agreed to take Deven's help. With the help of Deven her work was completed quickly. Deven's closeness to Nalini started growing later that day. Deven helped her in her office work when needed.

They leave the office together when they are discharged in the evening. Both came to Mumbai central and boarded the same local train.

Nalini was calm, silent first. But there was a tweet after Deven came in contact. She started laughing and speaking. One day while returning home, Deven spoke the Nalini, " Tomorrow is an office holiday. Let's go to Juhu tomorrow evening".

Nalini accepted Deven's offer.

Rain starts on sunday morning. It seemed like looking at the sky, the rain would not stop today. If the rain continues like this then it will be difficult to get out of the house. But raining stopped suddenly at four in the evening. Deven left the house without a moment's delay.

The rain had stopped but the sky was cloudy. Lighting was flashing. The clouds were thundering. Only water was visible on the roads. Rain had destroyed the daily life of people. Deven got of the bus on Juhu and stood on the side of the road. Very few people were seen on Juhu due to rain. Traffic on roads was much less then other days.

In such a bad weather, he had little hope of Nalini coming. He thought call Nalini. But by doing this he thought better to wait. After some time a bus stopped in front of him. Nalini was the only one who came out of it. Deven smiled at her, as soon as, he saw her.

"How long have you been here?" Nalini asked.

"Not much", Deven said while holding Nalini's hand, "I did not expect you to come in such a bad weather. In such a bad weather, the house holders could refuse you to go out of the house.

"There is no one to deny me. Here I am alone", Nalini said. While holding Deven's hand and walking with him. "I promised to come to you. How can I not come".

"You never told before that you live here alone".

"Never had such a discussion. Then how do I tell you this".

'In such a big metropolis, the parents agreed to leave you alone?"

"It has been many years since my parents passed",

"Sorry", Deven said regretfully, "Why haven't you married yet?"

"I am married".

"Are you married?" Deven looked at Nalini by surprise. Signs of married woman were not visible on her body. Nalini understand the intention of seeing Deven. So she said, "I am also divorced ".

"Divorce?" Deven spoke with surprise after listening to Nalini', Which fool divorced such a beautiful woman? Who is a cruel person who has been done such a thing to you?"

"He didn't. I had given divorce to Venkat." Nalini strongly spoken.

Nalini at this time seemed like an incomprehensible puzzle. He considered her a virgin girl. But she was abandoned. She doesn't bloom, was a crushed flower. He was close to her for the last several months. But did not know the truth about her. He started looking at her with a questioning point of view.

"I tried hard not to divorce him. But ..." Nalini was strangled.

Venkate drinks alcohol. I had come to know about this honeymoon. But I didn't mind it. Now a day the prevalance of alcohol has gone too much. He comes home drink every night. I would help him change clothes. I would feed him with my hand. Slept with her at night. In the morning when his intoxication had subside, I used to explain it with love. Tells him about the harms caused by alcohol. Convince him not to drink alcohol. He listens carefully to me but . . .

Nalini suddenly stopped speaking. There was a silence between the two far a whole. After some time she again started telling.

Earlier Venkate used to pay money for household expenses. Gradually he kept paying down. And then closed. Now he would not even listen to me. His drinking habit was increasing day by day. After all, I also had a stomach and I also needed other requirements could have been left. But bread was needed to fill the stomach. When I told him about my needs, he said. "Many people who throw money on your youth will be found. Find something similar for you.

Nalini's eyes filled with tears coming from her own past.

"Today I know the reason for your sadness and silence". Deven said.

"Now when Venkate came drink, I started fighting with him. One day he came home after drinking a lot of alcohol. I said something in anger. He was upset to hear me. He pushed me out of the house and beaten me in front of the people of the colony. If he had beaten me indoors, I might have tolerated. But I could not bear the open disrespect. There was only one way to avoid everyday quarrels and insults. And I divorced him.

Nalini became silent after telling her past. Nalini's face turned white Deven did not think, it was right to scrape Nalini's sad heart. That day both returned to their respective homes.

Deven and Nalini's relationship started to intensify after that day. They started getting closer to each other. They both spent a lot of time together after office. They spend the whole day of office holiday together. Eat and drink together. Shopping together and watching picture. Enjoying the cool sea waves in the evening.

There was a three day holidays on the festival of Dussehra. He asked Nalini to walk to Khandala. Nalini agreed to go with him. Many people come here during holidays. That's why hotels and tourist homes fill up. Like how they got a single bedroom in a hotel.

During the day, thay roamed together and had a lot of fun. Sleep in the same bed at night. Sleeping on the same bed in a room, how long the physical distance between them. Could last? They had already come close to their mind. The physical distance between them was also reduced.

The evening had set in. They were both walking along the sea shore. Nalini said seeing Deven silent, "What are you thinking?"

"I've been thinking about telling you one thing for several days", Deven said, "But afraid to tell you".

"You are afraid to tell me? Am I ghost or Don?" Nalini blossomed after hearing Deven.

"You are not a ghost or a Don but I am afraid that you do not deny". Deven said seeing Nalini running with him.

"Before you spoke, you took fear in your mind", Nalini said, "First say. After all, I also hear what you are afraid to say".

"Let's sit first'.

The Moon came out in the sky, while clouds strewn across the sky. There was a game of eyeballing between the clouds and the Moon. The milky light of the Moon spread all around. The sea was calm. Deven and Nalini sat on a rock that was submerged in half the sea.

"Now say what you want to say". Nalini said.

"I want you. Love you".

"Just afraid to say so much", Nalini without hasitation said, "I love you too"

"Why this distance when we both love each other? I did't want to be alone anymore. I want to marry you. Marriage is necessary to honor love in society. Marriage binds man and woman in one thread. Marriage gives freedom to love man and woman".

"Deven, I do not agree with you", Nalini strongly spoken, "I love you too. I am not yours by heart. I'm yours even with my body. If you don't want to be alone, I'm ready to be with you. We can live together in live in relation. But do not want to get married".

"Why?" Deven said after listening to Nalini, "When you are ready to be with me. Why are you refusing to marry me".

"I want to return to Venkate". Nalini had such expressions on her face, as if she is remembering Venkat. Her eyes looked distraught to find some one.

Nalini had come to close to Deven that he felt her like an open book. But today her words made her a mysterious woman again. Nalini divorced Venkate. But today she was talking about returning to him.

Deven did not understand so he said, "You divorced Venkate yourself and now you ...?"

"I have divorced Venkate but I have not forgotten him. No woman forget her first love. Venkate was the first man in my life". Nalini said, "My friend Padma from Chennai called me. Venkate is very sad and misses me so much. I always pray to God not to give alcoholic husband to any woman. The blame was not on Venkate but of alcohol. Who would care for him now?. How lonely would he be without me?" One day he will realize his mistake and he will come looking for me."

Lines of depression erupted on Nalini's face. Deven had heard of the woman's sacrifice. But today idol of love and sacrifice was siting in front of him.

"Deven if I marry you and if Venkate ever comes, I will not be able to return with him. I will be very sorry that I will not be able to be your wife in this birth. But I will pray to God to make your wife in the next life. Until Venkate comes to pick me up, I am ready to be your without getting married".

Deven started looking at Nalini. The love of south Indian beauty was divided on two sides. She did not even want to forget her past. And the present also did not want to let go her hand.

There was immense water behind Nalini's back. Her eyes could see more depth than sea water.

Martyr

My limbs are relaxing. Mouth dry and my body is shaking. The gun is going out of my hand. What is the benefit of a such war in which a family member has to be killed. Make your own sister a widow. No... No... I can't bear the sin of widowing my sister. Whether he kills me. I'm ready to die by his hands.

Relations between the two neighboring countries were not normal. Firing on the border. But love does not see enmity nor does it accept the bond of religion, caste or boundry. No one knows when to fall in love with whom.

A sister she had a great attachment to the internet. Everyday a lot of her time was spent on the net. One day on facebook she became friends with B of neighboring country. After friendship, they both started chatting daily.

They fell in love while chatting. Their love rose so fast that they decided to become a life partner. One day she said while talking her brother about her love, " I want to marry B."

"You have gone mad? Do you even know what you are saying? The neighboring country is our enemy and you are dreaming of living with the man of the enemy's country" After listning to the sister, A said. "Forget him. Think of making another man your life partner.

"How is the relationship between two countries. What does love have to do with it? Love is a matter between men and women. Sania is also married to a man from a neighboring country". Giving some examples she said, "If I get married, I will do it from B. Otherwise I will remain a virgin for life". A had no one in this world except his sister. A had to bow in front of sister's stubbornness. A married her sister to B.

The relationship between the two neighbors was not good. The rulers of both countries did not let any chance of spewing poison against each other go away by hand. The people of both countries also looked at each other with unfaithful eyes. The media of both countries used to add fuel to the fire.

No matter how tense the relationship between the two countries. Brother- in-law, brother in law had tremendous love. B comes to A with his wife on the festival of Rakhi and Diwali. A did not forget to visit his sister and brother-in-law on Holi. They never faced any kind of trouble when they went to each other's country. They got a lot of love from the public. They both used to kill each other and were ready to do anything for each other.

Seeing his brother-in-law B in front, Alowered his gun. "No. I won't kill my brother-in-law". He murmured in his heart and decided to flee the battle field. He was about to turn from the battle field to flee, that his conscience sounded.

"What are you doing?"

"I will not fight a war", Asaid.

"Why?" his conscience asked, "come to fight then why won't you fight?

"If I fight, I have to kill my own loved one. I have to kill my own brother-in-law". Asaid again.

"Forget what Sri Krishna preached to Arjun in the field of Kurukshetra. When the consience reminded him, he remembered the teaching of the Gita.

"Arjun, who born, his death is certain and after death rebirth is also certain body dies, not soul. Soul is immortal and indestructible. Why do you grieve? Don't feoget you are a warrior. Kshatriya's religion is to fight. If killed in battle, you will get heaven. If you did not follow the kshatriya religion and ran away from the battle field. You will be defame. Defamation is worst than death.

A's steps stopped as soon as the teachings of the Gita came into focus. He thought. I am standing in the battle field as a soldier of my country at this time. Soldier religion and duty is to fight. The soldier standing in the battle field in front of the soldier is not his brother but his enemy. He picked up the gun as soon as this idea came to mind. Asaid while pointing his gun towards B.

"I know that firing on you means making my sister a widow. But before the sister, my duty is to the motherland. The mother who gave birth to me. Pose me up. I will not let the enemy's nefaricus steps fall on my motherland. Protecting the motherland is more important than protecting the honeybee.

B said after listening to A, "I also know what is means to shoot at you? Snatch her brother from sister. But this time you are standing in front of me not as my brother-in-law, as enemy soldier. As soldier of the country from the enemy".

Aand B said after listening to each other, "Let us do our duty towards the motherland.

A and B gun fired simultaneously ... and ...

Incomplete love story

"Went to Switzerland to have a honeymoon".

"Honeymoon", listening to Vibha, Anu hesitantly said, "Go after marriage ".

"You? did not see you before", Manav said after seeing an unfamiliar girl in the drawing room.

"This is Anu, my aunt's daughter. Came yesterday night'", Deepa walked in to the drawing room before Anu could speak. She spoke while introducing Manav and Anu to each other, "This is Manav, Rajan's friend".

Anu ca me to Jabalpur for the first time with her mother. Some thing happened in Anu's heart during her first meeting with Manav. Manav's charming personality impressed her. The same happened with Manav.

Earlier Manav used to come to his friend Rajan's house after many days. But after meeting Anu, he started coming every day with some excuse. One day Manav said to Anu, "Do you have come to Jabalpur for the first time.

"Yes". Anu responded with a shook neck.

"Bhedaghat, Gaurighat, Madan Mahal are manymythological and historical sights here.

Manav took the responsibility of showing Anu to Jabalpur. He takes Anu daily wherever Manav goes with Anu. Deepa also used to go with them. Deepa was Anu's age. While walking with them, she understood that Manav and Anu were beginning to love each other. Even then she sobbed Anu's heart one day. After knowing Anu's heart, Deepa told her aunt Radhika about Anu and Manav's love.

Manav compeleted software engineering. He was selected in a multinational company on the college campus. He had to go to Mumbai to join duty after two months. Manav was handsome. He belonged to their caste and he was also employed. What could Radhika then object to her daughter's love? When Radhika talked to her sister. Nita said, "Manav is a good boy. He is Rajan's friend. The family is well known. If Manav and Anu want each other, then there is nothing wrong in their relationship".

Nita and Radhika went to Manav's house and talked to his parents about Anu and Manav's relationship. Manav's parents had no objection to the son's choice. Anu and Manav are engaged after both families agree.

Anu returned to Delhi after a month. But she did not come alone. She brought memories of the moments spent with Manav to her heart. They started talking on the mobile every day. They were lost in love for hours. And then Manav went to Mumbai.

During the day, Manav did not get time to talk due to work. But at night he did not forget to talk to Anu. Both of them kept talking till late night.

Time passed slowly. After passing B. Tech. Anu was also selected in a multinational company in Mumbai. Radhika does not send her daughter far away. for a job. But Anu's fiance was already there so she agreed to send her daughter.

Anu had informed Manav about her arrival. So Manav came to the station to take Anu himself. Anu started living in relation with Manav.

The company of Manav and anu was different, but the time of office was the same, so they used to go out of the house together. On sunday there was an office holiday. They enjoyed the day completely. They used to go on the beach on a holiday. They would enjoy the cool waves while sitting on the beach. Days passed by.

Manav and Anu lived in the same room under the same roof. How long could be physical distance between them last. One night Manav held Anu's hand and pulled her towards him. Anu said while trying to get out of his grip, "What are you doing?"

"Love".

"Right now you don't have the right to love me like this".

"What did you mean?" Manav said after listening to Anu.

"We are not married yet." Anu was not ready to surrender before marrige. Manav said while explaining to Anu. "We are not married but are engaged. If we have grown up, we will get married one day. What difference does it make if both of us have to become husband and wife. We make physical relationship before marriage or after?"

Anu thought on Manav's explanation. What difference does it make when she is to be married to Manav. Physical contact is made before or after marriage. And this idea came to her mind, Anu surrendered.

Sex is also an addiction, like smoking and alcohol. Once addicted, it does not stop. After that night, Manav and Anu started living as husband

and wife. She was believed that marriage is a ritual to show society. If a man-woman wants to live like a husband and wife without performing the ritual. Now the courts are also recognizing such relationships.

And slowly the cycle of time started. Anu was happy with Manav. Her days were spent laughing and smiling. One day Manav returned from the office, then there was a young woman with him.Manav said before Anu could ask anything about that young woman, "She is Shreya. Today she has joined my company. She has came from Delhi. She will stay with us till there is no arrangement."

Shreya wasmore beautiful and flamboyant thenAnu. She wasmore modern and open minded than Anu. Shreya was attracted to Manav in her first meeting.

Manav used to leave the house withAnu earlier but now he started coming with Shreya. He used to return home early in the evening. But now comes late night with Shreya.

Anu's ears became alert on seeing Manav's growing affection towards Shreya. One day she said while explaining to Manav. We are engaged. So it is not right to take interest in Shreya.

"You know she works with me. She is staying with us. If she comes with me. If she laugh with me. What is wrong in this?"

Anu had explained Manav with love several time, but Anu's explanation did not affect him. Anu understood, Manav by taking more interest in Shreya and seeing his day-to-day activities. If she does not do anything quickly then he will get out of her hand.

What to do? How to saparate Manav from Shreya. After much thought, Anu took leave and went to Delhi.

Anu did not hide anything from her mother. All things were clearly told. After listening to the daughter, Radhika kept thinking for a long time. Then she talked to her sister Nita on the phone. Nita went to manav's house after listening to her sister. She spoke to Manav's parent. After much deliberation they asked Panditji and after a month fixed a wedding day of Manav and Anu. Nita called Radhika and told her to get ready for daughter's marriage.

Anu called Manav when the wedding date was set but he did not pick up her phone. Anu was very angry at this act of Manav. She murmured in her heart, "Let us get married. Then I will see you?"

Despite being angry with Manav. She was very happy when she came to Mumbai from Delhi. Why would she not be happy. Manav was going to be her forever.

After getting off the train, she looked around. She came to Mumbai for the first time. When Manav came to pick her up. This time she reached home alone. After reaching near the door of the house she stumbled. The lock was hanging on the door. Today is sunday. Where did they go this morning. Thinking she took the key out of the purse. She also had a key for lock. Anu keyed in the lock but lock did not open. She was surprised, why did not the lock open. She looked carefully and found out. There is another lock on the door. Why? She did not understand. But she understood that this work was done on purpose. Then Anu came to notice of Vibha living in the front flat. She asked Vibha, "Where is Manav and Shreya?"

"What?" listening to Vibha, Anu said with surprise, "what are you saying?"

"Manav and Shreya have gone to Switzerland for honeymoon. The reality is telling you."

"But after marriage . . .?"

"You are right, go for honeymoon only after marriage". Vibha said, "yesterday both of them married in the court and went for honeymoon at night."

Knowing the truth from Vibha, the ground got out from under Anu's feet.

Anu went to get the wedding date to make Manav her own. But Shreya married Manav without making a date. Manav was engaged to Anu but got married to Shreya.

Anu felt cheated. She was badly defeated by surrendering to the faith of marriage.

Saw eyes

"No . . . No . . . No . . .

Eva had come from Itly to visit India. Her friends who had visited India earlier said, that, "foreign tourists are not safe in India. Taxies and police also not trust worthy".

After visiting Delhi. Eva was supposed to go to Agra. She asked the hotel manager, "How many hours Bus took for Agra?"

"By the way bus takes four hours", hotel manager replied, "But it is winter season. Fog is also very much. So it may take six to seven hours".

According to the six hours, she had chosen a 12 O'clock bus at night. Despite having fog on the way, the bus came to Agra in four hours.

The bus took her out of the gate of ISBT and went to head. She was the only one who came out of the bus. It was four O'clock in the morning . There was silence all around.

Unknown country, unknown place, she was alone in the silence of the night. She had engaged guide before leaving Delhi. She called the guide but his phone was switch off.

Two autos were standing outside the bus station. Seeing Eva getting of the bus. An autowala jumped on her. Seeing him coming towards her she panicked and shouted loudly. Inspector Dinesh was on guard. Hearing her cry he immediatly reached near to Eva.

"Miss what happened?"

"No . . . No . . . " Eva started running away after seeing Dinesh.

"Miss don't afraid. I'm police." Dinesh show his Identity card.

Seeing the Dinesh's Identity card, Eva could not believe him, she did not know english as well fearing she was running away.

Dinesh had called the ladies police and translator by calling the control room. Police also tried to call her guide too.

What Eva heard from friends proved to be wrong. She was very impressed with the work of the police.

She was thinking as she walked of Police station with her guide.

"Not heard by ears truth is what is seen with eyes.

Little light

Tapan was surprised to see the lock on the door. And old man came to him before he thought anything or got any other question in his mind. "To whom you want to meet?"

Tapan said, "Nazma".

"Nazma has become the principal of the college. She lives in a college bunglow." The old man told about Nazma.

He boarded the cab again.

He came to Delhi to meet the publisher. After visiting the publisher he went to Agra to meet Nazma. He spent many years in this city. He saw the changes in the city from childhood to youth. Some sour-sweet memories were also associated with this city. Whom he could not forget even after wanting. After thirty years he came to this city. Thirty years is enough. The city must have changed a lot in the last thirty years. Many classmates could still meet ; but he didn't want to find anyone. What did he do by searching? When there was no contact in the last thirty years. He did not even have contact with Nazma. Still he came to meet her. And he reached Nazma's bungalow's. He asked the woman cleaning lawn, "The principal is?'

"You have to talk about admission", the woman said after listening to him, "She does not meet at the bungalow. You meet in college."

"You go and tell her. Tapan has come", That woman went in.

"Tapan . . . you . . ." On hearing Tapan's name, Nazma came running. The gap of thirty years does not diminish. Tapan was middle aged. Nazma was fat as she was middle aged. Her eye sight was also reduced, so she started applying glasses.

"Thank God you recognized me. I think you forget me.'

"Where are you for so many years?" Nazma could not control herself seeing Tapan after many years. She cried and wept. In this way someone goes away? For thirty years you did not even try to know whether I am alive or not? Was this your love?" Nazma kept crying and not knowing what she said? Tapan stroked her back. Nazma was silent after losing her heart.

She wanted to say something after separating from Tapan, then Tapan put a finger on her lips, "Do you intend to return me from outside?"

"Sorry", Nazma realized her mistake. Nazma took Tapan in.

"You sit. I make tea." Nazma went to the kitchen. Tapan thought.

"I Nazma. I also study in this college". Tapan studied inAgra college. One day Nazma came to him and said, "Read your poem in newspaper. Touched heart".

Tapan was fond of writing poems. His poems was also published in newspaper. Nazma was quite impressed by reading one of his poem and went to meet him. Both became friends in the first meeting.

"Nazma was impressed by Tapan's simplicity and personality. Tapan was impressed by Nazma's beauty.

After becoming friends, they spent a lot of time together.

They both spend the college holiday together. Sometimes they go to Taj Mahal, sometimes Sikandra, sometimes Sikri. They both sat for hours on the side of the Taj. They both eat and drink together and watch the picture. As time passed, Tapan fell in love with Nazma. One day they were sitting in the Taj garden, then Tapan said,

"I've fallen in love with you."

"Me too." Nazma spoke on hearing Tapan.

"I want to make you my life partner."

"I'd love to be your wife."

"Our religion is different. Will your mother be ready for our marriage" Tapan expressed doubt knowing Nazma's heart.

"My mother is a woman of open thoughts. She does not believe in caste, religion, high and low. She should not mind our marriage."

Nazma's mother Zarina was a teacher at school. She was a open minded woman. She did not impose any kind of restriction on her daughter, gave her all kinds of freedom. She fulfilled her every wish. She had no objection to friendship with Tapan. So Nazma thought that her mother would not be against her marriage to Tapan.

But Nazma's thinking turned out to be wrong. Zarina was a progressive woman with open thoughts. She was in favour of woman's freedom. She was in favour of giving woman equal rights as men.

But, her daughter wants to marry a Hindu man. She got upset after hearing this. On the matter of daughte's marriage she remembered religion, caste and everything. She spoke after listening to her daughter, "Is there a famine for Muslim boys, so you want to marry a Hindu boy?"

"Marriage is not between Hindu and Muslims. A man and woman are married.

"Man are in all religions. Muslims also have. Then why from Hindu man?"

"The woman should marry the man whom she loves. I love Tapan."

Nazma tried her best to convince her mother. But in vain. She did not listen. She spoke to daughter in clear terms, "I will not do your marriage to a Hindu."

"Mom, if this is your stubbornness, then listen to mydecision too, listening to her mother, she also said in anger, "I will marry only Tapan or else I will remain a virgin for whole life."

Nazma had told Tapan about her mother's decision. Tapan said after hearing that, "Now".

Mother loves me a lot. I will convince her. But it will take time.

"What are you thinking?" Nazma brought a tray of tea. Seeing Tapan immensed in thought, she said.

Tapan said, while returning from past to present, "Those old memories."

"Have tea?"

Tapan said while drinking tea, "Where is mother?"

"It's been ten years since she died."

Tapan regretted hearing the news of Nazma's mother.

"Where are you?" Nazma asked.

"I went to Mauritius thirty years ago. I am there."

"Don't you want to come here?"

"No", Tapan said while drinking tea. "Even if I want to come. People of there will not let me come. They love me a lot."

Nazma and Tapan were talking about what happened to them in the last thirty years. Telling each other.

Tapan suddenly asked while talking, "You got married?"

"Wedding?" Nazma said after listening to Tapan.

Nazma had tried hard to convince her mother, but Zarina was not ready to marry her daughter to Tapan.

Tapan get a job as soon as college was completed. He get a Hindi teacher job in Mauritius. He went to Nazma before leaving Agra. He told Nazma, "I want to make you mine."

"I tried in every way, but my mother is not ready to marry you.

"So we take another way. We do the court marriage."

"I love you deeply. You are the first and last man to come in my life. I will not let the other man in my life. But I will not be able to rebel against my mother to marry you."

"Nazma I don't understand the definition of your love."

"When I was a little girl, then my father died. Mother was young. The whole life was in front of her. She could have married another if she wished. But she did not do this keeping in mind my future", Nazma said, "I love my mother very much.

"I will not be able to marry you by rebelling against my mother. But this is not mean. I will marry another man. I will only marry you."

Despite Tapan's much pursuasion, Nazma was not ready to marry him by rebelling against her mother. Then he left angry with Nazma.

Therefore, he never wrote a letter, nor called, nor did he ever try to know about her. Tapan was extremely upset with Nazma but he did not forget for a single moment. Nazma was the first woman to come in to his life. And who forgets his first love.

At night, Nazma made food and placed it on the table. Tapan said looking at the dishes, "Have not fotgotten my choice yet."

"You were the first man to come in my life. How can I forget moments passed with you. Your like and dislike."

Years later, some one had fed with so much love. He ate to much in taste. Laying in bed at night, he spoke to Nazma, "Ask one thing."

"What?"

"You loved your mother very much. So by revolting against your mother. You did not get ready to marry me. Tapan said, "But after your mother passed away, there was no hindrence in our marriage?"

"No."

"So you could come to me or call me."

"I thought so but . . .

"But what?" Tapan said on seeing Nazma leaving the matter incomplete.

"You were angry with me, so I thought. You must have forgotten me or you got married."

"So you did not trust your love." Tapan said after listening to Nazma.

"I had definitely gone away from you. But didn't go alone. I took your memories with me. I did not forget you even for a moment. I keep your memories in my heart every moment."

The night was moving slowly. But they had no sleep. Two separated lovers who met after years. The talk of both them was not ending. And after a long time. Nazma asked,"When will you go?"

"Day after."

"Have met after so many years and will leave so soon." Nazma said after listening to Tapan, "Won't let you go so soon."

"Thirty years ago. I went alone. But now I will not go alone." Tapan said, "Take you with me."

"Taking me along?" Nazma spoke with surprise.

"We already wanted to be one, but your mother did not let it happen. And I could not take you with me even I wanted to, but now I will not listen to any of you. You will have to walk with me."

"At this age our marriage." Nazma spoke with surprise after listening to Tapan, "What will people say?"

"First your mother did not let us have one and the entire youth went out alone in loneliness. Now for fear of people, if we do not unite, we will never be one."

"Now what is the benefit of our union at this age. I'm a twinkling lamp now. There is not much oil left in this body lamp. Do not know when this lamp extingnishes."

"I live in the dark. There is darkness in my life. If you come to light for some time in my life, then I will consider my life blessed."

Nazma was hesitant about marriage at this age. Fear of what people would say? But agreed to Tapan's explanation.

Even though she has lost her age. But at this age, she felt thrilled to imagine herself getting married and moving with her husband.

Life and death

sound.

"Ghir . . . Ghir . . . what happened?

Several voice emerged simultaneously when the Marador halted with the

"I see." the driver said while coming down.

Nigeria was in the grip of civil war for the last several years. The country was in a tizzy, a rampage. They had become enemies of their own, so every moment there was a danger of death.

People were being killed every day in a mutual struggle. Nobody knew who would die. Most of the villagers had fled due to fear of death. Some people did not leave the village in the hope that one day the condition of the country will improve and peace will prevail again. But instead of improving the situation, things were getting from bad to worse. To avoid the danger of death on his head every time, the remaining people in the vgillage decided to take refuge in the neighboring country of Libya.

The Libyan border was three hundred kilometers away from the village. They could not go so far on foot. The villagers talked to many bus and tractor owners, but no one was willing to risk their lives due to the rampage in the country. After much effort a Matador person agreed to take them.

The matador in which twenty people could come in fifty people, including old, young, children women entered like sheep-goat. They went at night. The weather was very pleasent at night. There was cool cold wind. But the Sun had crossed the sky halfway. And now as matador was growing up. The heat of the Sun was increasing. Heat waves, flying sand dunes and hot sand. In such a situation, the journey of the Sahara Desert was very difficult. But in the hope of life, they were ready to bear all the sorrow and pain.

They were all afraid while walking through the village. The fear of death in their hearts could be read clearly from their faces. As they passed away from the village the fear of death diminished. And after years the beauty returned to their faces. Having come so far from the village, they were all assured that they would not die now. But suddenly the Matador . . .

"Look like it won't be right", the matador did not start even after a long time with the driver and cleaner, then an old man said.

The Sun was blowing fire in the sky. The water they carried was over. Sunshine, heat, heat stroke, sweat coming out of body and dry throat due to thirst. The second old man spoke, "If we keep standing here everyone will die.'

And the convoy of the fifty people, walking in the hope of living in the Sahara Desert.

The Libyan border was still thirty kilometers away. No village could be seen till far. There was no tree, where they stayed for a while. There was no question of getting water in the desert. On those fifty people, two women also had newborns.

They fled their country to escape death. But does death leavs the chase. Crossing the Sahara Desert, due to heat and thirst, people kept falling one by one.

Life doesn't stop for fear of death. No stop even for the dead. They kept moving forward looking at the deceased.

Out of fifty, only six people had crossed the Sahara Desert to Libya after enduring sunnyheat and thirst.

Frost

Raghav was very fond of travelling abroad. He went to China for tourism. He wanted to see the ancient and historical places of China. He hired guide Elice.

Elice was tall and fair complexion. She was pretty. Was a magic in her voice. She looked like a heroine.

Elice was showing Raghav different historical location of China. They were together for several days. So they both get mixed up and started talking like friend.

One day both were talking. She spoke,"Chinese girls like Indian youth very much."

"Why?" Raghav looked at Elice with questioning eyes.

"Indian youth have big eyes while chinese youngester have small eyes like a elephant. Indian youth have long face while chinese have round." Indian youth have pointed noise while the nose of chinese youth is flattened.

While making physical comparisons of Indian and Chinese youth, Elice told why chinese women love Indian youth.

"Then you must also like Indian youth." Raghav asked her.

"Yes.", Elice said, "Indian youth are handsome and attractive. I like them too."

"So would you like to marry an Indian young man?"

"No"

"Why not"? Raghav was surprised to hear Elice, "When you like an Indian man then why don't you want to marry an Indian man?"

"Indian youth looked beautiful and smart until they get married. But some times after marriage, they looks thick and ugly."

Hearing the praise of Indian youth from Elice. Raghav had a hope in his heart to make her his life partner.

But don't listen to her. Broken his heart.

Seed

"Here should be a temple for worship."

Acountry was burning in the fire of civil war. people of different religions were living together for centuries. But how did the battle of religion erupt and people became thirsty for the blood of people of another religion?

Seeing the fire of hatred, the whole country was engulfed. The whole country was hit by violence. The Government and administration were helpless. They were not able to understood what to do? Why not? After all they were the same people in government and administration. who were in society and country.

People had lost faith in each other. So no one felt safe. No body knew when friends should become enemies. When, who is killed by whose hands? In such a situation some wise people decided to leave the country.

Hundred people leave the country and go out by sea. When they were going by ship, one of them shouted, "Look at that".

It was a deserted island. After discussion with each other, those people decided to settle on that deserted island.

Every one was very happy by settling on this island. Every moments in their country, there was a danger of death on their head. There was no fear or danger here. All were living together with love and affection. There was no conflict of religion.

"Tomorrow another will say here should be Maszid." hearing that man, the head of those people said.

"What is evil in this?" Maszid is necessary for prayers".

"Then the demand for church and gurudwara will also arise here."

"When people of different religions are living here, different places of worship will be required for them."

Meaning the quarrel that caused us to migrate from our motherland. You want to sow the seeds of that quarrel here too.

Humsafar

"Wear it." Seeing her chill with cold, taking off his overcoat and giving it to her, he said, "If you get a cold you will fall ill."

"Let it be cold. I will die at least." She said while chilling with cold" "No one in this world is crying for me."

"If no weeping will die."

Taking his overcoat with his hand, she said, "And you?"

"Give up my worry, I'm a soldier. What is cold and what is hot for military. "

And she wear his overcoat taking from his hand.

He was going to the village for the first time after his mother passed away. Mother waited impatiently for his arrival. Many days before, she started preparing for the joy of the son's arrival. She used to prepare dish of his choice. Whenever the son comes home on leave. She didn't forget to say, "Get married now".

"I will do. But let the girl, I like meet."

"This is what you say every time you come home on leave", mother would get angry after listening to him, "Will you bring a bride after my death?"

And mother's statement came true. Mother had left this world before his marriage. He did not feel like going to village. What will he do by going to the home which is closed? He thought about going some where else. But where? He could not think. And instead of going somewhere else, he was going to his village.

The young woman in the front seat was depressed and deep in thought. There were different thoughts in his mind on seeing that girl. After several hours, the train stopped, then after thinking about the idea that came in the mind, he got up and said her, "Come, let's go."

"Where?" she asked with surprise.

"Your home . . . "

"My home?" When she understood the meaning of what he said? She said with a squid laugh, " If you know my past, you will not even bring the idea of making me to yours into your mind."

"Your . . . past . . . "

He was going to his village by Sampark Kranti train. The train stopped at a small station due to lack of signal. When the train left the station, the young woman came running and climbed into the moving train. Four men came running after her. They had sowrds and poles in their hands. But the train had left the platform . So they could not hold this young woman. They stood at the station and kept looking at her.

Recalling that scene he spoke to her, "You have left your past behind. Who missed? Why do you want to remember that?

The young woman listened to him and watched. Her future stood before her.

And without delay for a moment, she walked with him.

Moan

"A bullet would kill me too . . .

Jamila was shocked to hear the news. She could not believe that her son could do this too . . .

Her son Zaheer was a player. A player of the cricket. He used to go out of the village. Whenever he used to go out of the village he told the mother. Jamila would never stop her son from going. He used to come back whenever he went to play outside the village. But this time . . .

Like every time, this time also he had spoken to the mother before leaving.

"Am I going to play the match".

Zaheer had gone to play but joined the terrorists. He had turned from player to terrorist.

Jamila strongly hated terrorists. Whom she hated. The son had become that.

Jamila husband Naseem could not read and write. Even though he was illiterate and uncouth in the eyes of world. But he was a firm patriot. He loved Kashmiriyat and hated terrorists. By the way entire Jammu and Kashmir region was affected by terrorism. But the most affected area was the border area from the neighboring country. There were training camps of terrorists every where in the neighboring country. Training was given to become terrorists in these camps. Some young people from our country also used to get misled by the terrorists. These people were sent to the neighboring country after crossing the border to take training. There was tremendous vigil and security at the border.

The border area was so-inaccessible due to being surrounded by high hills, deep trenches and dense forests that it was not easy to cross through dodging security forces yet when some terrorists were sucessful in infiltrating.

terrorists took refuge in villages near the border. Some people gave them shelter in the greed for money. Some people gave them shelter due to fear, threat. Whenever the security forces got information about the terrorists hiding in the village. They used to come and surround the whole area. Security forces frequently encounter militants in this area.

Apart from terrorists, separatists were also active in the valley. They also had the support of the neighboring country. They received money from the neighboring countries and Gulf countries. There was an alliance between terrorists and separatists. The money come from foreign countries was used by separatists to protest, to shut down the lives and spread unrest. The saparatists had formed groups of stonemasons as well. People were associated with these groups by giving fear of religion and greed for money. These groups were associated with social media. Security forces when encounter terrorists, then the saperatists would send message through these groups. As soon as the message was received, a large number of people reached the place of encounter. These people started throwing stones at the security forces. The attention of the security forces would have gone to the other side when the stone was fired. Taking advantages of this terrorists sometimes managed to escape.

For the last several years, there was an atmosphere of unrest in the state. Therefore there was no new industry in the state. Those who were old were also closed. Business was stalled due to the day's shutdown, demonstration and protest. The main trade of Kashmir was tourism. Due to the arrival of tourists, the valley was vibrent. Hotels, Shikaras, travel agents, shopkeepers, horse holder etc all had their livelihood from tourism. Due to terrorist incidents, the number of tourists visiting the valley was declining day by day. The country was suffering from the problem of unemployment. Secondly unemployment was also increasing due to decreasing number of tourists. Many unemployed were seduced by separatists. These people used to prepare for protest, demonstration and throwing stones after taking money.

Naseem was a labourer. The deteriorating situation in valley had also affected him. He too did not get work every day. Some times he did not get work for many days. He was also lured by the saparatists for money. Naseem was a true muslim. Even if he does not offer prayers for five times, but believed in following the path of Allah. He loved to starve but not to do wrong things. So he did not come under the greed of separatists.

Some villagers were influenced by the ideology of the separatists. When terrorists were trapped under security forces, these people used to give them shelter in their homes. But Naseem was not among those people. Once a terrorist escaped from the security forces and reached Naseem's house. He appealed to Naseem to give shelter in the house. But Naseem shouted at him and said, "I will not let your nefarious steps in my house".

The result of Naseem not giving shelter, the terrorist shot dead by security forces.

The terrorists were irritated by Naseem on the death of his partner. They started thinking of Naseem as their enemy. One day many terrorists came to his house. They forcefully pulled Naseem out of the house. All were imprisoned in their homes for fear of terrorists. One of them said while pointing a gun at Naseem, "Do you know the consequences of enmity with us."

Jamila ran to save the husband. She lay down on her husband. But the terrorists forcefully pulled her apart. Jamila kept crying, begging for her husband to leave. But the terrorists had no effect on her crying, pleading. They shot Naseem.

The son, who had killed her husband, became their companion and she could not believe that her son could do so.

After the murder of the husband, the responsibility of raising the son came on her. When the husband was alive, she never went out alone. But she had to get out of the house to work after her husband murder.

Zaheer was fond of cricket since childhood, watching TV. When he was young, he used to play cricket with the children around. In school he became the captain of the school team. On growing up he formed his team with boys from the near by village. He started going to play matches outside the village with his team. He would have won the prize if he had won.

Seeing her son playing cricket, Jamila also got fond of watching matches on T.V. She would watch the crickters on T.V. She also sees that after winning the match, the players are getting rewarded from place to place. People are crazy about the players. They are getting love and affection of the people. The country is getting praised abroad. And Jamila also started dreaming of his son's beautiful future.

She thought. One day her son will also become a big player of cricket. Her son's photos will be printed in the newspaper. He will also be seen on T.V.

People will be crazy about her son. Her son will also have his name abroad. People will say how well Jamila has raised her son even if she does not have husband. People will respect her along with her son.

The dream she had been seeing for years, the son shattered in one stroke. The terrorists who murdered his father. The son become their partner.

Will she be respected, in her society, community and village. Patriot father's son traitor. people will curse him. Will look at her with disgust. Seeing her they will taunt her. "Look terrorist's mother?"

Hearing the burning and taunting of people, it will be difficult for her to get out of the house. And how will she respond to her husband by going to God. What was lacking in her upbringing. The son who did not follow in the foot steps of the father had joined the terrorists. Hearing the news of her becoming a terrorist, she started mourning.

Had to go then he would have gone. But he would shoot me. one shot before leaving. So that I don't live to see his hands stained with blood of innocents. Patriot's son traitor? I would not have lived to hear this. Had to kill me, I would not have to see a soot on my son's mouth. You left but I was left to die as a mole after ridiculing people. If you were to become a terrorist, you would start by sooting your mother. Then you will know how much pain and sorrow he must have whose own is killed by a terrorist shot. It was better than such children, I would be childless. Atleast this day does not have to be seen.

Jamila was mourning over son's becoming a terrorist. Someone made a video of her on mobile. This video went viral and Zaheer also watched it.

Mother had brouhght him up after suffering so much pain and hardwork day and night. as soon as this was noticed the gun handed over by the terrorists was released from his hands.

"Mother . . .

ran to the house saying mother.

Love Across the Sea

"I'm gonna be a mother".

As soon as Sandeep took mobile in hand, he sees Julia's message. After so many months?

Seeing Julia's name, his eyes flashed. The face blossomed as if some one had got separated after years. The page of her past fluttered open as soon as he remembered Julia.

Trin... Trin...

Hearing the voice of bell, he was awakened. He looked at the clock. It was five O'clock. Who can be at the door so early morning? He didn't want to get- up. But he had to get-up.

As soon as he opened the door. He saw the young girl. Seeing an unfamiliar foreign young girl he surprised, 'To whom you want to meet?"

"Rohit", she said.

"Who are you? How do you know Rohit? Why do you want to meet Rohit" he asked the girl several questions at once.

"I am Julia from Phillipines", She said while introducing herself, "Rohit is my facebook friend".

Rohit and Sandeep were friends. They both served in the passport office in Srinagar. Rohit was very fond of friendship. He also had many foreign friends on social media. They lived in the same flat. But he never interfered in his personal life.

Rohit was a resident of Lucknow. His Father died a few months ago. Mother lived alone in Lucknow. She lived sick. So he had his transfer to Lucknow.

"Where I will stay now"? Julia spoke sadly after listening to Rohit's transfer. "I wanted to surprise Rohit. So I did not tell him about my coming here".

"What happened if Rohit is not here. I'm his friend. Don't worry. I'm here". Sandeep said seeing Julia sad.

Sandeep brings Julia in the room. After sitting her he went to the kitchen and made tea. He said while giving tea to her, "Drink hot tea".

They were talking while drinking tea. After drinking tea Julia went to the bathroom.

Sandeep called a Texi. He took Julia with him to Pahalgam and Sonmarg.

Seeing the natural beauty of Kashmir Valley, she was enchanted and said, "Really, If there is a paradise in the world. So here it is".

They returned home late at night. Julia said as soon as she come in the house, "I am tired want to sleep".

"You sleep on the bed, I will sleep on the floor below". Sandeep lived alone so, he had only one bed.

"Why below? No. We will share the bed".

Julia was really tired. She fell asleep as soon as she lay on the bed. Sandeep was also tired. But he had no sleep. How can he sleep? For the first time a young girl was sleeping next to him. The heat of her body warmed the blood running in his veins. His desire to enjoy Julia's body **arose**.

He knew that it would be wrong to do so. So he tried his best to keep his mind under control. But all in vain. And he put his hand on her chest. For a while he lay calm when there was no movement in her body. Then his hand crawled over Julia's body. There was also fear in his mind while doing this. His actions can also cause some trouble. He had not even able to meet her properly in some hours. Knowing everything he could not stop himself from doing so.

All of a sudden Julia's eyes opened. Seeing Sandeep's action she got furious, "What are you doing? Making a lady hospitable and then playing with her honor. Is that your tradition? This is Atithi Bhavo"

After listening to Julia, Sandeep felt as if lot of water had been poured on his head. He said apologizing to Julia, "Sorry".

"OK", She forgives Sandeep for his repeated apologies.

Julia fell asleep again. But his eyes were awake to get her body, he did a stupid act. He fell into his own eyes. How will I get my eyes in the morning. What she will think about him. He does not know when he slept?

"Get up Sandeep. Drink tea", Julia was awake early. After making tea she raised Sandeep. She probably forgot the incident at night. Sandeep also did not mention that event After drinking tea, they agreed to go.

Sandeep had taken her to Nishat Bagh and other places. They were sitting in Shikara in Dal Lake. He purchased many items and gave them as a gift. They returned home late at night. Today Julia looked absolutely changed. She said as soon as she lay on the bed, "My flight is in the morning".

"So early? We haven't even been introduced yet, stay here a few days more".

"No. Sandeep. I have booked ticket. My Visa is also ending".

"Don't worry. I am, will make all the arrangements". Sandeep urged her to stay a few more days.

"No Sandeep, won't be able to stop now. I also do job. So I have return tomorrow".

In just two days, Sandeep had come so close to Julia, As if she has known her far years. Hearing of Julia's departure, he said in sadness, "I will not forget you".

"No body remembers. Every one forgets as time passes". Julia reacted.

Some people are not forgotten. You are the first woman in my life. I will never forget you.

And Julia left. He missed Julia. After reaching her country Julia forget him. No phone. no message.

The tone of her voice was telling, so excited to be mom. Sandeep said while attending her pleasure, "when did you get married "?

"Marriage? No. I did not marry." Julia said after listening to Sandeep.

"Did not get married"? Sandeep said with surprised, "Then Baby"?

"O...o...h...o"? Julia said when Sandeep's words were understood, "In our country a woman can become a mother without marrying. Such woman are called single mothers. I will become single mother."

"But some one will be the father of the child"?

"Is it necessary to mention father's name"?

"No, if you do not want to tell then let it be."

"I don't mind to tell. But knowing the name of the child's father you will not believe."

"Why I would not believe? Only woman can tell, who is the father of her child .? Sandeep said.

"So listen. My child's father is you." At last Julia said.

"I?" Sandeep spoke with surprise.

"Yes you", Julia said, "Forget what happened between us that night"?

Sandeep remembered that night when Julia reminded.

Sandeep was sad to hear about Julia's departure. Seeing him sad Julia takes him in her Arms and kiss his lips. At first Sandeep was stunned by Julia's unexpected behaviour. Then he also kissed Julia's lips. Sandeep looked into Julia's eyes.

Last night he tried to get Julia. Julia then scolded him and said to lot. But tonight she was ready to surrender herself. Julia's gestures boost his courage. And the distance between them disappeared. Two bodies become one. Remembering that night Sandeep said, "You won't be a single Mom."

"Means"? Julia said.

"This child is ours. You mother I father. I want to make you mine, will you marry me"?

"Really"? Julia speakes with surprise after listening Sandeep, "In our country, It won't happen men play with the body of the women, but avoid taking the responsibility of father".

"What happenes to women in your country. It won't happen to you." Sandeep said, "First we will get married. Then you will be mother. I am coming to pick-up you."

Julia did not even think in the dream this will happen.

She started dreaming of her future with Sandeep.

Banyan

"Birthday of tree?" Birthday of this Banyan tree . . .?"

There was a park in that area. A banyan tree in that park. Some say this tree is twentry years old. Some say forty while some fifty years old. But there were some people who said that it was even older. Everyone had different estimates and claims about the age of the tree. But no one had proof or evidence to prove his claims and estimates.

This city is counted in the big cities of the country. There are many defence material manufacturing factories of the Government of India, in which thousands of people work. Apart from being a center of religious faith, this city is also a tourist destination. Religious, tourist and historical places like Bhedaghat, Gaurighat, Chaurasi yogini, Madan Mahal are in this city.

With the change of time the development of the country gained momentum. The city also started developing along with the country. With the opening of the regional office of the railways, many private companies started knocking in the city. New educational institutions and factories are opening in the city. People started coming to this city for education and employment with the arrival of people from outside, the population of this city started to increase. New colonies started coming up in the city to provide housing to the growing population. The builders started building, flats and apartments from place to place. In order to provide housing to the growing population of the city, the Development Authority also decided to form a colony. This outskirts of the city was chosen for this purpose.

This area was densely forested with thousends of trees of different species. Land has to be acquired to build a colony. There is a lot of trouble. People whose land is acquired. They have to pay compensation. Many people who are not satisfied with compensation or do not want to give their land.they sue in the court. And it takes a long time to get decision from the court. So that the whole plan hangs in the balance.

But the place which was chosen by the Development Authority to form the colony was the place of Forest Department. The Development Authority and the Forest Department are both government department. So there was no problem in acquiring land to build a colony.

There was thousands of trees in the place chosen to build the colony. Cutting of trees was banned. Trees could not be cut without the permission of the ministry of Environment and Green Tribunal. Before cutting the tree it was necessary to got permission from them. There was both government departments to obtain and give permission. Hence, it did not take much efforts to get permission. After completing some formalities, the Development Authority got permission to cut trees with certain conditions.

After getting permission, the process of cutting trees starts. Small, big trees were cut down. Shrubs began to be cleaned. There was also a huge and dense banyan tree in this forest. In the afternoon, the laborers used to sit under this tree and eat and rest. The children of the laborers under the tree used to play and sleep. Sitting under this tree, officers, engineers and employees of the Development Authority used to work. The banyan tree was protecting all the people working here from Sun, heat and rain. So, despite cutting all the trees in the forest, that tree survived.

After the forest was cleaned, the process of building a colony started. Hundreds of houses were built for every income group. With the passes of time, the colony became ready. After the colony was formed, a park was built for the people. Who lived there. The banyan tree that survived the felling became part of the park.

The colony was formed but it was far from the old city. The station, roadways, hospitals, schools etc. were all away from here. Public transport equipment rickshaws, tempo etc. were not easily available. So, initially some people who had their own vehicles had shown interest in buying houses here. After the Development Authority's colony was built, many builders also built colonies around. After passing the National Highway many educational institutions, hospitals and companies office opened. People started coming to live in private colonies. Then the Development Authority colony also started populating.

With the passes of time slowly, the area which was previously deserted for twenty four hours. Where there were dense forests and people were afraid to come even during the day. That area was resplendent round the clock. The means of transport, rickshaws, tempo etc. were available all the time.

Earlier the park was empty. But after the settlement in the colony people started coming for a walk in the park. Only a small number of people used to come in the beginning. Gradually their numbers started increasing. Earlier people from this colony used to come. Later people from other colonies also started coming.

People who roam the park made many trips to the park. When they got tired, they would sit on the plateform made under the banyan tree. sitting here they would discuss topics like politics, inflation, rising petrol prices etc. During the day, children would come to play. They play cricket, football and others games. When tired of playing then they would sit under the banyan tree and relax. Except for a few hours of the night, the park was byzzing all the time.

Banyan tree was not only useful for humans. Birds also had their base on it. The mixed tone of different birds keeps echoing all the time.

One morning when Ratan lal came to walk, he brought bananas. He started giving bananas to everyone. Then kumar asked, "In which happiness are you distributing bananas today?"

"Today is my birthday."

Everyone came to congratulate Ratan lal on his birthday.

And after that day the tradition of celebrating birthday in the park started. Which ever birthday it was, he would bring fruits and sweets with him. Then everyone would sit on the platform under the banyan tree.

In honor of whose birthday it was, everyone would say a couple of words and congratulate him on his birthday wishing good health and long life. And they sit and eat fruits and sweets together.

One day they were celebrating Harish's birthday. When they were talking. Kumar said in the talk, "We celebrate the birthday of everyone by sitting under the banyan tree. But we do not celebrate the birthday of this tree.

Nakul spoke with surprise after listening to Kumar, "I have heard about celebrating the birthday of humans but have not heard of celebrating the birthday of the tree."

"You are right. No one celebrates the birthday of the tree."

"Why should we celebrate when no one celebrate the birthday of the tree."Mahesh said.

"The trees are not an enemy of humans. Friends of human beings. Trees consuming gas that pollutes the atmosphere. And trees give us oxygen gas which is necessary for our living. We get medicines, fruits and other daily necessities from trees. Which is so useful for humans. We do not celebrate his birthday.

"But the banyan tree gives us nothing to eat". Sudhir said,

" Why not give? Consuming polluted air, gives pure air. Its leaves are used to make utensils for eating food at wedding and other occasions. Its bank, milk, pots and coppals are used in Ayurveda to treat various diseases. In Hinduism, the banyan tree is considered a wish fullfilment tree". Kumar said while explaining the benefits of Banyan tree , "We sit and rest under this tree every day. Children get tired while playing, so they rest under this tree. We all celebrate our birthday under this tree. Which tree is so useful for us. Why can't we celebrate his birthday?"

"What is our fault in this? There is no tradition of celebrating the birthday of the tree." Shamlal said.

"There is no tradition but we can start." Kumar said.

Everyone had their own views and opinions. Some people agreed with Kumar's proposal and some disagreetd. A debate broke out our the tree's birthday. Kumar spoke about the usefulness of trees, religious importance and the utility of tree in human life. Kumar's arguments convinced everyone. All spoke in one voice, "The birthday of this banyan tree should celebrated."

"But when?"

After the decision to celebrate the birthday of the banyan tree, the question arose as to what day should his birthday be celebrated? No one knew what day the tree came out of the womb of the earth? When no decision of any day or date was made, Kumar said, "Tomorrow we celebrate the birthday of the banyan tree."

"Why tomorrow?" Naveen asked.

"Tomorrow is Buddha Purnima. On this day Gautam Buddha attained enlightenment by sitting under the tree. Should not this holy day is celebrated as the birthday of this tree?"

Everyone liked the Kumar's proposal. Funds were collected to celebrate the birthday of the tree. On Buddh Purnima, they all reached the park with fruits, garlands, sweets to celebrate the birthday of the banyan tree. Today the new tradition was about to begin. Untill now these people were sitting under the banyan tree and celebrating someone's birthsday. But today they were going to celebrate the birthday of the banyan tree. Everybody come thinking in their mind. What they have to say today? nature, environment, religious, importance of trees, utility of trees on similar topics, they came by preparing to speak. Everyone was happy. They were going to start a new tradition.

But as soon as they reached the park, they were all shocked.

The banyan tree of which they were about to celebrate his birthday, could not bear the velocity of the fierce storm that came in the night.

Was uprooted and fallen to the ground.

One arrow two prey

"Who?"

"David".

"The door is open. Come in".

David entered Sujata's call in the room. The room was empty. Seeing Sujata in the room, he walked to the bathroom door. Bathroom door was also open. Sujata was in the bathroom. He turned back as soon as he saw Sujata. She stood naked under the shower. Seeing David retreating she said. "Why shying? Come forward".

David walked to the door.

"Say. What's news".

"The boss is still unconscious". David told about his boss.

"It is good for us if he not come in sense".

"What does you mean?" David said after listening to Sujata", I did not understand.

"What doctors do if a body part gets rotten?" Sujata answered David question by question.

"They cut that limb from the body and separate it".

"Correct. Absolutely Correct' Sujata said while praising him," You are sensible. Boss is also like that . . . if he regains, consciousness then, we will no longer be anywhere. So don't let him come to his senses".

"I don't understand what you say? Say clearly".

"The boss is in the police possession. Police was searching the boss for a long time. Now he is in the police custody. The boss is old now. His body is not stagnent. If he disclosed all the secrects under police pressure we would all be caught".

"You are right" David said", Then what we should do?"

"Kill him before he regains consciousness".

"What are you saying?" David spoke with surprise. "You are his lover and saying such".

Sujata was standing under the shower. She was nude. Tiny little drops of water were falling on her head. And sliding on her nude white body.

"I never liked your boss. I was married to someone else. But you kidnapped me before I got married. You did not make me your own but gifted. me to your boss. I never liked boss. Still continued be a victim of his lust. Now there is no use repeating old things", Sujata said", You will be the boss when the boss dies. Everything will be yours when you became a boss. Me and my beautiful body will be also yours".

David saw Sujata standing under the shower. Seeing her bare beautiful body David's blood running his veins became hot lust in his eyes Body ripping lugs. Sujata reads his feelings and said", No need to get excited now. As' long as the boss is alive. I'm his. First do what I said. Then me and my body is yours.

David was the right hand of the boss. Boss does any work must take feedback from David. The boss belived on David a lot. David never thought of betraying his boss. But gets ready to betray his boss to make Sujata his own.

At night while the world was sleeping. There was silence all around. The policeman deployed to watched the boss was also sleeping. David then entered the room through the window. David killed the boss by strangling the pillow. After that David calls Sujata", Boss in no more".

"Well done", Sujata' said", Now I'm yours for ever. Come soon. I'm waiting for you in bed".

Sujata body made him crazy. He was eager to reach her. But Sujata told the police. about the murder of boss. Police quickly came in action. Police chased David. David falls prey to the women's trio character and was shot by police.

Sujata was a clever woman. So she hunted two birds with one stone.

A Unique Solution

Ila was the most beautiful girl in the city. Along with winning the beauty queen award in the college. She also won the title of the most beautiful woman in the city. Hundred of young men were fond of her beauty. Every young man extended a hand of friendship towards her. Every young man had expressed his love and said to her", I want to make you mine".

"Sorry. Ila gave the same answer to every young man", I accept your friendship but do not approve of becoming a wife".

But Sandeep was lucky in this matter. Sandeep and Ila become friend. With the passing of time they came so close that one day Sandeep proposed marriage while expressing his love. Ila accepted his proposal without any delay. And they become husband and wife. Ila was born into a wealthy family influenced by western culture. She got all kinds of freedom from her parents. As a result, She was not a archaic as a common Hindustani girl. She was an open minded girl influenced by western civilization, culture and ideas. She considered marriage to be necessary. But marriage did not mean that she should be tied to a man for whole life. She considered marriage not a sacred. bond but a compromise.

Even after marriage there was no change in the living, behavior and habits of Ila. She did not stop going to club and parties. Even after marriage, there was no shortage of her male friends. She met each friend warmly. She would laugh and talks to her friends. She had also illegal relationship with some friends. Marriage in India means the bonding of Woman and man each other for whole life. Husband can never tolerate that his wife laugh or has sexual relation with other man. Sandeep also started feeling bad. He explained to his wife, "Ila now you are married. So now it is not good that you laugh, speak or have physical relations with other man".

"I married you that does not mean that I have become your self for the whole life", Ila said, "When I stopped you? No matter, how many women you have sex with. I don't mind".

By all means Sandeep tried to teach Ila to be in the dignity of the Indian woman. But all in vain. Ila had completely differed view of life. She considered life like a flowing river. She did not believe in living life like the stagnant water.

When Sandeep was a virgin, then he dreamed. His dream was a beautiful educated wife. On seeing Ila for the first time he become obessed with her. The making of Ila his life partner came in his mind at the very first meeting. He prayed to God in his heart. And God has heard his prayer. And one day the beautiful girl of the city became his wife.

He was very happy to have a beautiful girl like Ila as his wife. But his happiness could not last long. His life became hell by making a beautiful woman his wife. The family members objected to Ila's open thoughts and friendship with others men. Sandeep friends also started taunting him.

After listening the taunts of the people. Sandeep was so upset that he decided to commit suicide. One day Sandeep went to leap from the top of the mountain with the intention of suicide.

A woman was already present at that place. Sandeep said after seeing her "Have come to commit suicide? Not knowing suicide is a sin".

"Ooo Hoo . . . you are giving me advice", listening to Sandeep the woman said sarcastically", Why you have come here?"

"You are to right. I too have come here with the intention of commuting suicide", Sandeep said after listening to that woman, "First you tell me why do you want to commit suicide?"

"My name is Rachna", And Rachana started telling her story to Sandeep", I was born in a middle class family. As soon as I stepped on the threshold of youth. I also dreamed of my future like every virgin girl. I too had a dream handsome husband. Who loves me, my home and children Just as I saw in my dream, I got. My husband Ramesh was a engineer. I did not love any man before marriage. My husband was the first man in my life.

I heard before marriage that Ramesh does not have any bad habits. But after coming in-laws it was revealed that the husband had a habit of drinking alcohol. He also had illict physical relations with many women. A large part of his income was spent on alcohol and other women.

I tried to convince my husband with love and lead him on the way when he is not drink. I would love to explain him. Ramesh promised me he will not do this now. But he forgets his promise. He has short of money to give me, but not for other women. In our country after marriage a woman's home and world is her husband's.

After marriage a woman lives only by being loyal to her husband. This is what she wants from her husband. No wife can bear that her husband is related to other women. I also did not like that my husband would fly with the other women. He did not believe in love, then I started trying to stop him from quarreling. He got angry with this and started saying, "Who are you gonna stop me?"

I could not get my husband on the right path. The people started taunting me.

"How is the wife. Who could not control her husband?"

From husband, and I'm fed up listening to the taunts of people. That is why I came to commit suicide. "Why do you want to commit suicide?" Rachna asked.

"Your story matches my story. You are upset with your husband. I from my wife".

"Our story has similarities", Rachna said after listening Sandeep's story. "You are right".

"Can't there be a solution that we don't have to commit suicide?"

"Think. What can be done to solve this?"

Sandeep and Rachna started thinking. After some time both speak together.

"There is a solution".

"What?" Sandeep asked.

"We should get divorced from our life partner".

"Your decision is correct".

"So let's stop commuting suicide".

"Now we should walk from here", Rachna said.

"But let me say one thing before returning", Sandeep said.

"What"? Rachna asked him.

"If we had not met today we would have commit suicide".

"You are absolutely right".

"So why we don't give our lives to each other".

"How?" Rachna asked.

"Why don't we hold each other hand for whole life".

Rachna started thinking Sandeep's proposal. After thinking for a while. She said,"I accept your proposal". "Let's go now". Sandeep extended his hand towards Rachna. Rachna hold Sandeep's hand.

And they have to return to start a new life.

The night of her decision

Was the last night to decide. Lajjo was avoiding daily. But now the postponement deadline was over. She was to be testified in court tomorrow.

Tonight she had to decide what she had to say in court tomorrow. She was the only eye witness to murder of Saudan's nephew. Her testimony was to decide the life and death of. Saudan, She knew that if she told the truth in court, the courts would sentence Saudan to death. If she lied in court, the court would leave Saudan. He would be saved from hanging. Saudan death and life was linked to her future. If Saudan gets death penalty, then she will be widow. Her vermilion will be wiped, bangles will be broken. If Saudan remains alive. She will not be widow, with the life and death of Saudan there was a decision of to be her widow or not.

Tonight was the turning point of her life. She got lost in the past before deciding what to say in court tomorrow?.

Saudan was a resident of Nagla. As a child he learned to steal. He was caught several times and had to be beaten while stealing. He became a well known thief. When he grew up he stopped stealing in the near by village. Now he started stealing away from his village and state. He used to do this so not to get caught. Whenever he had to steal he would leave the village for a few days. He used to go to the new city. every time to steal. He used to steal so smartly that to never got caught.

A dark night of winter, old house in the outskirts of the city. Saudan as soon as entered that house he realized that the house was empty. Still he was careful and alert. Saudan crossed a long corridor in the dark and reached a room. Night lamp was on in that room. He stunned seeing the scene of that room.

There was a young lady in that room. Her hands and feet were tied and cloth was stuck in the mouth. She was filtering to get free As soon as she see Saudan in room, She was horrified. The fear on her eyes and face was appearing. He could not under stood any thing. He stood in a confusion for a while, seeing him standing like this, She was convinced. Then she prayed to be freed from the direction of her eyes, Saudan understood her gesture. Saudan asked while freeing her, "Who are you?"

"I'm Lajjo. I'm a poor girl. I have no one in this world".

"How did you come here?" Saudan asked her.

"This is Thakurs bunglow. Thakur enjoys here. His men bring a woman everyday for him. Today they have brought me forcefully".

"Where is Thakur?"

"He may come at any time".

"It means we should get out from here quickly".

The path through which Saudan entered the bunglow brought Lajjo along with him.

"I'm a thief. I went to the bunglow with the intention of theft. I didn't stole any thing. But brought you out of Thakur's cluche. Now you are free to go home".

"No. Now I can't go my house". Lajjo said'

"Why?"

"The woman whom Thakur likes. Does not leave her at any cost. Today he was going to play with my body. But I had good luck, you saved me before I became a victim of Thakur's lust. I won't see him. He will search me. What will he do with me if I get caught again, you may not imagine?"

"Then what you want?"

"You have saved my honor today. If you do not come . . . Now I give myself to you".

"What are you saying?" Saudan said after listening Lajjo.

"I'm telling the truth. If you want to save me from the clutches of Thakur. So take me with you".

Saudan got confused after listening to Lajjo. After thinking for a while he brought Lajjo with him. After reaching his village. He advised the elders. On their advised he married Lajjo.

After marriage he gave up his illegal work. He started doing odd jobs. But he did not get much money in these works. So he started farming with land at half share. A few years later, he took a loan from the bank and bought a land.

And he started farming in his own land. Saudan was young and healthy. In the lonely moment's of the night, when he used to touch fingers on Lajjo's young body, the strings of her body rose. Her desires wakes up as soon as the husband comes to contact. Saudan would awaken her lust but he couldn't calm down. Lajjo gradually understand that Saudan is not a man.

Saudan also came to know about his deficiency.

Sex is needed, just as bread is necessary for stomach hunger. Likewise sex for body. Her husband could not calm her body's hunger. So she leaned towards chagan.

Chagna was Saudan's nephew. Saudan agriculture field was far from his home. So he would leave house in the morning and returned in the evening. Lajjo would remain alone in home. Chagan used to came Lajjo's house everyday.

Chagan nature's was funny. He kept on joking with Lajjo. But she didn't make fun of him and sometimes. She even scolded him. But after discovering her husband's physical weakness. She also opened up to him. She also started joking with him. Changing behavior of Lajjo encouraged chagan. The result of this was that earlier chagan used to joke with his mouth. But now he also started molesting her.

Gradually they came so close that one day chagan caught Lajjo as soon as he got chance.

"What are you doing this?" "Love".

"You know what is our relationship".

"At this moment, there is only one relationship between us. I'm a man and you are a woman", Chagan said, "When man and woman meet in private, then you know what happens?"

"What happens?" Lajjo asked in a naughty style".

"Tell you", Chagan starts undressing Lajjo's body. Lajjo understood what he wanted to do with her. But to show she started protesting. On that day Lajjo's physical connection was established with Chagan. She felt a new joy for the first time after marriage. Her sex desired fulfilled and she got full satisfacion. After that day Chagan and Lajjo started playing sex game whenever they got chance. The happiness She didn't get from her husband was getting from her nephew.

One day Saudan went to the city to buy seeds and other goods. Chagan arrives after Saudan leaves the house. He drags Lajjo into bed. They both started playing sex game.

By the time Saudan reached the bus stand, the bus had left. So he returned home. On reaching near the house, he heard the sound of laughing. Saudan thought, When Lajjo is alone in the house whose laughter then?

To know who is inside, he crossed the wall and entered in his house. Seeing the inside scene he was shocked. Lajjo and Chagan were absored in the game of lust. He lost his senses after seeing this scene. He got so angry that he cut Chagan head with a shovel.

Lajjo ran away seeing her husband. Saudan ran and hit her. She screamed loudly. People gathered to hear her scream.

In those days police station was not everywhere. Police station was in the nearby town. Someone went there to gave information.

When anger subsided Saudan thought about what he did. He will surely be punished for this act. To avoid pusishment he erased all the evidence. Police arrested Saudan.

Thakur and Mahajan agreed to give witness against Saudan. They were not present at the time of murder. Lajjo was only the eye witness of Chagan murder. In the court Saudan Succeed to prove Thakur and Mahajan false. Now trial rested on Lajjo's testimony.

Night was passing slowly. Lajjo was thinking about what she had to say in court tomorrow. Saudan rescued her from clutches of Thakur. Supported her and got married her.

Her religion was to be faithful to her husband, but she did not. She commited the sin of having a physical relationship with a other man. The result of this sin was Chagan's murder.

If she tells truth in the court then her husband will get the death penalty. And she will become a widow. She will prove to be rascals in the eyes of people and she will lost her honor. She did not want this happen with her.

At last she decide that she will be loyal to her husband.

She will tell in the court that Chagan wanted to rob her honor, her husband tried to save her. Chagan was killed in this attempt.

Price of one night

"Come".

Saira wins Anurag's heart by coming into the bedroom. As soon as she in bed, She invited Anurag to come soon too. Anurag stood near the bed and looked at saira's snug beauty.

Saira's personality was very attractive, Fair complexion, long black hair, thin nose, lips like rose petals, slim waist, her body was so sexy that looking her naked body. Anurag body began to tremble the ears heatup. The body started to become to uncontrollable due to excitement. And he jumped to bed. He kept playing with Saira's body till late night. Fell asleep when tired.

The sound of the shower coming from the bathroom in the morning opened Anurag's eyes. As soon as his eyes opened, he stretched both arms and took full action. Saira may have gone to the bathroom to have a bath and freshen up. Anurag was thrilled remembering the night's bedroom scene.

Once again his mind started to make saira his bed. To fulfill his heart's desire he waited Saira to come into the bedroom.

Yesterday he left office and went to see the picture. English movie was very hot and sexy. Anurag was very excited to see the scenes of picture on the screen. It was ten past night after coming out of the cinema hall to the station.

There was no much congestion on the platform. Passengers in local trains are significantly reduced during the night. He was waiting for the train. Then a young woman came to him and said softly, "let's".

"Where?" Anurag was surprised to hear that young woman.

"Wherever you want to take?" She said with a smile.

Listening to that young woman Anurag understood she does business of the body.

Apart from chklaghars in Mumbai, such women are easily found on the sea shore, parks and other public places. Anurag came to see hot and sexy picture effect was still on him. He was excited. His wife went to her mother's home. So he could not calm his excitement with his wife. After watching the picture his body was hungry. So he accepted the woman offer.

She joined Anurag as soon as he said yes. Anurag lived in Andheri. He took her to his house. On the way Anurag asked her, "What's your name?"

"Is it important to know the name?"

"No. But what harm in telling?"

"My name is Saira".

"Where you live?"

"Not at one place".

Remembering the night, his heart broke agian. He wanted to enjoy her fair beautiful body again. Seeing Saira not coming out of the bathroom, he got up from the bed with the intention of grabbing her there.

The bathroom door was open and the shower was on. If Saira in not in the bathroom. So where she? He searched the whole house but could not find her. If she is not at house. Where did she go?

Then suddenly he looked at the paper kept on the table. He read it.

You fully enjoy my body at night. Taking the price for that pleasure. By the time you wake up, I have gone too far to trap another man in my web.

He immediately searched his house after reading that paper. Fifty thosands rupees and his wife's gold ornaments were kept in almirah, was not there.

Anurag got confused after discovering the theft. Did he write a report to the police. But how to tell the police? He himself had brought Saira his home to enjoy her body.

He was most worried about his wife. What would he say to her? If the wife finds out the truth. He will fall from her eyes.

What an expensive price he had to pay for getting the body of another woman for one night.

Don't Leave me alone

And when the time was over, his Mangalyan was ready to return, as soon as he got the command from the Earth.

"Bye", Manav spoke to that woman. "Now it's time for me to return".

"Leave, me alone?" the woman said.

"I don't want to leave you alone. But what I should do? I am helpless. This Mangalyan only take me back".

Manav was sent in Mangalyan. After many days, Mangalyan had landed safely on Mars after covering a long distance. Then the door opened and Manav took the first step on Mars.

"Wonderful- - - amazing- - - wonder- - - amazing- - - "Manav jumped with joy, as soon as, he stepped on Mars. Why not happy? He became the first man to come from Earth to Mars. His name was recorded in History. As soon as he landed on Mars, he started completing his mission. He was moving forward collecting samples from mars. Then his eyes fell on the woman.

"Woman?"

Mars is deserted and uninhabited. Here comes the dust strom. Scientists believe that may be there in no life. But is life possible can life flourish there? Some scientists believe that our ancestors came to Earth from Mars. Everyone has their own guesses and fantasies.

The planet on which there was no possibility of human life. Woman on that. Its meaning was clear. Any other country on Earth had secretly carried out the Mars mission. That country had sent woman of its country before the arrival of Manav. From which country did this woman come?

Manav stepped forward to know this but stopped after a steps. The face and figure of that woman was not looking like the woman of the Earth at all.

Is she from another planet? Seeing that woman, Suddenly a thought came in mind of manav. When this thought came to mind, he looked carefully at the woman standing in the distance. She was an alien of another planet. He got scared when he believed it. That woman can also harm him by considering him as her enemy or rival.

And where Manav was, he remained standing.

Perhaps the same thought had come to that woman's mind as well? And her moving steps had stopped. For some time both stood apart and looked at each other. They started gesturing to each other from a far. After sometime when they were convinced that both of them would not harm each other. Then they came close. Humans from two different planets met on the third planet. They started talking after greeting each other by raising their hands.

But?

From two different planets-different language. They both could not understand each other language. Then they resorted to gestures and sign language.

"When did you come here?" Manav asked that woman.

"A few hours before you arrive".

"My mission is for twenty four hours. After twenty four hours this Mangalyan will take me back to Earth". Manav asked, "And yours?"

"My mission is also only four twenty four hours. But now I can hardly return from here?"

"Why?" Manav looked at the woman in amazement.

That woman took Manav to her Mangalyan and started explaining in signs "When my Mangalyan", touched the surface of Mars, there was a severe storm here. Whose grip got damaged my spacecraft and lost contact with my planet. I survived- - - But my craft?

"O- - O- - H- - O" Manav said with regret, "I'll see".

After inspecting her spacecraft the Manav said, "It's destroyed".

After spending sometime near the craft, both of them started completing their mission.

Mars had high mountains. Was a rough ground. Mars seemed to have a lot in common with Earth. But they had not yet-seen any signs of life. May be their spacecrafts have landed in the desolete and uninhabited region of Mars. Is there life like Earth on Mars? This could be known only after seeing the planet Mars completely. But there was every possibility of life to flourish on this planet.

Manav was thinking while coming towards Mars. How will be spent twenty four hours on an unknown planet in the farthest space far away from Earth? But on coming here a woman from another planet got such support that he did not even know when the time passed? with that woman he had also completed his mission.

"You know my Mangalyan has been destroyed. After many years of tireless work, Our scientists were successful in sending me from Saturn to Mars. But his mission failed. Hardly another spacecraft should be sent to find me. And even if it was sent, after so many years don't know?"

"You are right" Manav listened to her and said, "Then?"

"Don't leave me alone".

But Manav ignoring her words, kept the steps in his Mangalyan.

"How will I be alone on a desterted, desolete, stranger planet? You do not go. We will build a new world here". The woman looked at him with folded hands.

Seeing the pleading eyes of the woman, there was turmoil in Manav's mind. On the one hand was his mission for which he was sent from Earth. On the other hand, a women from another planet pleads.

And before the door of his Mangalyan closed. Manav jumped from spacecraft.

Manav took her hand. Both were watching. Mangalyan going back.

Remaining Memories

Ramesh was very worried about Suresh's arrival. What will Rama decide? Will she go with Suresh or prefer to stay with Ramesh? He didn't know what would be the answer to this question.

Rama could not believe that Suresh would one day come to Mumbai looking for her. So she was surprised when he came. Introducing Ramesh and Suresh to each other, Rama said "This is Suresh, my husband and this is Ramesh, I am living in a live-in relation with him".

Suresh thought a lot after hearing that Rama was living with Ramesh. His wife was living alone with Ramesh. If there is no blood relation between a woman and a man, then their relationship cannot remain merely formal. There is very little chance that they may not meet physically. So does Rama have physical relation with Ramesh? If so, would it be appropriate to take an unfaithful wife with him? Should he ignore his wife's relationship with a man other than him?

But it's not right for him to think so? What right does he have to expect loyalty from his wife when he himself was unfaithful? If he wants to take Rama with him then he has to ignore her relationship with Ramesh. If he raises the question of her relation with Ramesh, then Rama can also raise the issue of his relation with Uma. Therefore he thought it appropriate to remain silent on this subject.

Every night Ramesh and Rama used to sleep in the room. But tonight Rama slept with Suresh in the room and Ramesh had to sleep outside in the balcony.

There was no sleep in Ramesh's eyes. He lay in the bed listening to the whispers coming from the room. Rama was furious. What was she saying to her husband? Suresh was apologizing. This is the weakness of a woman. If a man accepts his mistake, then she is ready to forget everything. On being pleaded by Suresh, Rama not only forgave him, but also surrendered.

Suresh had scolded Rama on the honeymoon. Her body was not even touched. Uma had snatched her right. For years, Uma used to enjoy her right. Today after many years of marriage, Rama got the right of wife. Despite marrying Suresh, Ramesh got the opportunity to make Rama's body his own.

Ramesh met Rama while searching for a rented house in Andheri. Ramesh came to Mumbai after getting a job in a company. On coming here he was staying at a retalive's house. But for how long? As soon as he came here, he started looking for a house for rent. But wherever he went, he was disappointed. Wherever he went for the house, his bachelorhood came in the way. That day also he went in search of a house. The widowed landlady had two young daughters. That's why she refused to give the house to the bachelor Ramesh. He sat on the platform outside the house in despair.

Rama's story was different from Ramesh. She got married to Suresh as soon as she completed her studies. After marriage, Rama moved from kota to her in-law's house Jaipur. Rama's husband Suresh worked in a company in Ahmedabad.

Suresh had a charming personality. When he came as a bridegroom, Rama's friends praised her luck. Rama too was so happy on hering Suresh's praises. But her happiness could not last, Collapsed like a mound of sand.

On the honeymoon, Rama was waiting for Suresh in the honeymoon room. Suresh came late night. As soon as he came, he, spoke to Rama, "I didn't want to marry you but my parents forced me to marry you in the greed of dowry. Got married but will not be able to spend life with you".

On the first night, Rama was stunned to hear heart breaking talk instead of sweet words filled with love.

And giving up the shame, humility and elegance of the newly wedded bride, she said.

"Why married then?"

"It was my mistake. I'm sorry".

Saying this Suresh fell asleep. Rama shed tears all night.

Suresh went to Ahmedabad alone after marriage. Rama came alone from her in-laws house what Suresh told her, she did not tell her parents.

But neither she went to her in-laws house nor Suresh came to pick her up. Then the parents got suspicious. They had asked the daughter. Then Rama told everything clearly. Rama's parents discussed among themselves and decided to leave Rama with Suresh in Ahmedabad. Mother said while sending her daughter away from house, "No matter what you have to do try to make your husband yours".

Rama's father had left his daughter with Suresh. On coming here, Rama came to know about the truth of the husband, Suresh was in love with his workmate Uma.

Uma was not pretties than Rama. But she was modern and bubbly. She was also smart and frank.

Suresh did not like Rama's coming. He started abusing her as well as harassing her. Rama could not win Suresh's heart even after suffering every atrocity. Still she did not leave her husband's house. Then Suresh forced her out of the house. Then she returned to her maternal house.

She didn't want to be a burden on anyone, she wanted to stand on her own feet. So she tried and got a job in a company in Mumbai. Rama's parents did not want to send their daughter to Mumbai alone. But she came to Mumbai. She had meet Ramesh while looking for a house. No one was ready to give a house to a single young woman. The same thing happened today. Rama was first introduced to Ramesh sitting outside the house. Both of them told their problems to each others. Both had the same problem. Ramesh proposed hesitantly, "If you don't mind we both take the house together."

Rama was upset while looking for a rented house. But still she thought for some time and agreed to live in a live-in-relation with Ramesh.

Rama and Ramesh started searching for a house together and got success in the first attempt.

Ramesh and Rama started living together. Both used to work in different places. But their office hours were the same. So they used to leave the house together. But in the evening both would return after some interval.

They buy daily neccessities together. Ramesh helps Rama in getting the daily chores done at homes.

Earlier the day of office holiday was spent at home. Later they went far a walk.

At night, Rama slept in the room and Ramesh in the balcony. One day Rama suddenly got fever. She had to lie in bed for three days. Ramesh took leave from the office. He took Rama to the doctor. He served Rama all his heart and wealth. Rama was very impressed by this. When Rama's health deteriorated, Ramesh had slept in the room. When her health improved, he started going to sleep in the balcony, then Rama said, "Don't sleep outside".

On that day onwards Ramesh started sleeping in the room with Rama. Sleeping under a ceiling in a room, when the physical distance between them disappeared . And physical relation were established between them. One day after the passage of time, Ramesh spoke to Rama, "Why don't we get married?"

"Marry me?" Rama quote, "You don't know my past so you are talking about marrying me."

"What is your past. Never told you."

Rama told her past, hearing which Ramesh said, "what is the meaning of such marriage? you also forget him."

"I am actually married to Suresh. He may not want me but he has not divorced me yet I am still his wife from a legal, moral and social point of view."

"So you divorce Suresh. Then we will get married."

"I am not married to you but I am living with you like your wife." Rama said, What is the shortcoming which can be filled only after marriage. Now even the court have started recognizing live-in-relation."

After that day Ramesh never again asked Rama to marry him.

Suresh was in love with Uma and wanted to make his life partner. He went to his home in Jaipur when his father got a call. When he came to know about his relationship with Rama, he got furious. He refused to marry Rama. But his mother and other relatives forced him to marry Rama.

He got married but after marriage came to Ahmedabad such that he did not return home. His parents thought that with the passing of time he would accept the reality.

Uma was born in a poor family. As soon as she stepped on the threshold of youth, she started having colorful dreams of future life. His father wanted to marry her as soon as, she passed the intermediate. But she refused. She completed her studies by teaching tuitions to the children. And then she got a job in Vasan Company.

Upon joining the company, she came in contact with Suresh. And the both became friends. Suresh liked Uma in the very first meeting. With the passage of time, he fell in lovewith her. He started spending money and giving her gifts from time to time. Suresh started dreaming of making Uma life partner. But before this could happen, he got married. Suresh did not tell Uma about his marriage But Uma came to know about Suresh's marriage when Rama's father left her in Ahmedabad.

Divan chand, the owner of Vasan company, died suddenly. After his death, his son Dharmendra, who studied ahroad, became the owner of the company.

Dharmendra liked the beautiful and attractive Uma at first sight. Dharmendra made her his private secetrary. At first Suresh was happy when Uma was promoted. But later on seeing her growing proximity to Dharmendra, he became jealous. Dharmendra started giving her expensive gifts along with taking her on tour.

Seeing Uma's growing attachment to Dharmendra Suresh tried to understand her by referring to his love. But in vain.

Uma's longing was to live a life of prosparity and luxury. She was inclined towards Suresh to fulfill. her wish. Suresh's income was limited. He could fulfill her wishes to a certain extent. Dharmendra was rich and was able to fulfill Uma's wishes.

On his persuasion, Uma did not agree. So suresh rightfully tried to stop her. Uma got upset on this act of Suresh, "In what way do you want to stop me?"

"I want you. Love you".

"If you had loved me, you would not have married Rama".

"That was my mistake. I am ready to rectify my mistake by divorcing Rama".

"If you loved me you wouldn't have made this mistake, "Uma said," Now you are married to Rama. She is your wife".

Uma did not listen to Suresh. She married Dharmendra.

Uma's infidelity hurts his heartdeeply. He fell ill in her grief. He was admitted to the hospital for a long time. On recovery, he realized his mistake. Then he thought of Rama. And he went to her looking for her. Rama was surprised when Suresh arrived. He had absolutely no hope that one day Suresh might come.

Ramesh thought that Rama had forgotten Suresh. But if this had happened, She would not have spent the night with him in the room. Ramesh could not sleep the whole night thinking. about Rama.

In the morning Rama. said to Ramesh, "I have decided to go with Suresh".

"But Suresh turned. you down for Uma?"

"Uma got married. Suresh has also accepted his mistake".

"So you forgive him?"

"Yes Ramesh".

"You know very well I want you, love you and want to marry you too".

“I know everything. But I am not divorced. I am Suresh’s wife even today. He has come to pick me up. I am right to go with him”, Rama said while. explaining to him”, forget me and get married”.

Rama was gone. This house was rented by Ramesh along with Rama. They were living together even though there was no relation. While living, together, Ramesh started feeling that Rama is now only his. But today his illusion was shattered. Rama had gone with her husband. Only her momories were left with him.

Request for review

Thank's for reading my book, Don't Leave Me Alone

If yoy realy enjoyed from stroies of this book. I would be very greatful if you'd post a short review your support really does make difference and I read all the reviews personally. So I can get your feed back will try to make my next book even better.

Thank's again for your support and love to me.

Your's

Kishan Lal Sharma

E-mail : kishanlalsharma18750@gmail.com

Mob : 91-9760617001

About Myself

Name	:	Kishan Lal Sharma
Birth	:	18 July 1950 Mehsana (Gujrat)
Mother	:	Smt Chand Devi
Father	:	Sri Ram Pal Sharma
Wife	:	Indra Sharma
Education	:	(1) B.A. (2) Diploma in story & screenplay writing.
First Literary work	:	Rashifal (satire and taunt) published in Diwana Tej in 1978
Honours in the field of teaching	:	Vidyavachaspati by Vikramshila Hindi Vidyapeeth, Bhagalpur in 2014.
Writhing areas	:	Stories, Articles, Poetry, Novel, Laghukathya, Review etc.
Publications	:	Amar Ujala, Rajasthan Patrika, Ajit Samachar, Mukta, Saras Salil, Gahanachal, Aah Jindgi, Madhuri, Filmi Duniya, Madhumati, Sahitya Bharti, Veena, Naya Gyanodya, Giriraj etc since 1978 continously publishing.
Novel	:	Hara Hua Aadmi
Collection	:	Published in Laghukatha Sansar, Andhaimod, Bharat Nepal Laghuratha Darpan, Yadon ki Nagri, Boond Boond Sagar, Laghu ki Viratata, Kukubh and in more than 50 collections.
Book Published	:	Shesh jivan, Parde ke Piche
In Hindi	:	Me Dropdi nahi hoon, Neem ke ped, Ansuljha Prshan, Praye sparsh Ka ehsas, Khokhle hote Rishte.

Book Published in English	:	Don't touch me.
On social Media	:	(1) kindle :3 ebooks in Hindi and 2 in English on KDP. (2) You may also read me on Matruhharti, Hindi Prtilipi, Facebook, Whatsapp, Story mirror, Medium, Nojoto & my page and blog also
Awards	:	(1) First prize in Laghukatha Competition, organized by Gemini Academy in 2005 and third prize in 2007. (2) Consolation prize in the Laghukatha writing competition organized by samajik Aakrash on 2013.
Honors and felicitations	:	(1) Laghukatha Shilpi honour by USM Patrika in 2003 (2) Felicitations by Mahima Prakashan in 2006, 2007, 2011 and 2012. (3) Honoured by New Ritambhara Sahitya Munch in 2010 and 2011. (4) Sarswat Samman Conferred by Shabd Surya in 2008. (5) Sahitya Gaurav Samman by Sahitya Samman in 2017. (6) Shriram Thakur Dada honour Conferred by Madhya Pradesh. Laghukatha Parishad Jabalpur in 2012. (7) Rashtriya Sahitya Gaurav Samman conferred by Nirala Sahitya evam Sanskriti Sansthan Basti in 2012. (8) Shabd Saadhak Samman conferred by Nazar-e-Delhi in 2017. (9) Hindi sahitya siromani by Sahitya Mandal, Nathdwara

Originally belong to	:	Baswa (Rajasthan)
Present status	:	D.C.I (Hq)-Retired from Agra Division-NCR.
Present address	:	103, Ram swaroop Colony, Shahganj, Agra-282010.
Contact No	:	9760617001